IQ and the Y2K

A sci-fi comedy

David Abernethy

PRAXIS
BOOKS

IQ AND THE Y2K

ISBN 978-0-473-55188-9

Also available for Kindle ISBN 978-0-473-55189-6

Published by Praxis Books, Auckland, New Zealand
books@praxisgroup.co.nz

Produced for David Abernethy by AM Publishing New Zealand
www.ampublishingnz.com

Cover design by AM Publishing New Zealand
Cover image of Philips K9 television courtesy of the Collection of Toitū Otago Settlers Museum

Also by David Abernethy

The Prophet from Silicon Valley – The Complete Story of Sequential Circuits

IQ and the Y2K

This is what I've come halfway across the galaxy for.

– IQ, rev from Sirius C Major

PROLOGUE

It was just another insignificant speck of light far off in the endless backdrop of open space. You could quite easily miss it, as there were plenty of other much more interesting specks to look at. However, close up this particular speck revealed some extraordinary qualities. For a start, it consisted of a very special and rare element, but what really made it stand out from the other specks was the way it moved; it moved at a phenomenal speed.

In fact it hurtled. It had been hurtling mindlessly across the galactic void for some considerable time, completely oblivious of anything that might get in its way. And the interesting thing about moving objects – and it was certainly true with this one – is that the further they go away from some things, the closer they get to others. The longer this goes on, the more the object in question is pushing its luck.

Time is a wonderful thing, they say. And if there is one thing that space has plenty of, it's time. Indeed it was only a matter of time when proximity was going to catch up with all this hurtling and something would eventually get in its way.

The victim in this case was a medium-sized habitable planet which had been peacefully orbiting a G-type main sequence star for the last few million years or so. And, unfortunately, on one particular fateful day, it just happened to be in the way.

The object exploded impressively as it hit the planet's upper atmosphere. The centre of the explosion was as bright as the system's star, and the blast radiated out across the sky. Most of the object was instantly vaporised, and the small fragments blown clear continued their downward arc towards the planet surface, burning up along the way.

Once again, the proximity effect became important: anything directly under the blast was subjected to a thermal roasting, followed by a killer shock wave. Anything far away would have stopped what they were doing, looked up and said something like, "What was that?"

But generally, the planet wasn't overly bothered by it all; these things happened occasionally. And the planet had plenty of spare time on its hands anyway. It was going through its lazy, lumbering Jurassic period and took any unusual cosmic events with a grain of salt. Life was easy going there; animals, vegetables and minerals cohabited within a perfectly balanced ecosystem, and had long decided that the odd cosmic fireworks display was nothing to worry about.

Only one fragment reached the ground. By this stage, it was a fraction of its original size and with a rather subdued, almost anticlimactic end, smacked into the middle of a vast swamp, tossing up a huge wave of muddy water.

It had stopped. No longer free to whizz around the galaxy at breakneck speed, it was now locked into the confines of a rather soft and smelly prehistoric bog. The crater it had caused quickly filled with water, and once the last of the ripples finally died away, all was quiet, all was still.

Except for time, of course.

Time marched on, as always.

A few hundred metres away a group of mud-splattered sauropods went back to munching on some leaves.

Chapter I

They say the three golden rules in property investment are location, location, location. And often, an outlook to die for is also high on the list of priorities.

Right smack in the middle of Scorpius-Centaurus could therefore be just what you're looking for. Provided you're filthy rich, of course.

Indeed, the spacious lifestyle mansions, luxurious resorts and palatial getaways that had popped up across the great void between Perseus and Orion, numbering in their millions, provided that special place for the sole purpose of taking in one of the most awe-inspiring and impossibly beautiful spacescapes in the galaxy.

Right across the upper-left arc of Scorpius-Centaurus, viewers were bedazzled by an array of multicoloured galactic dust clouds, forever billowing and evolving, endless cosmic rays curving off into the ether, and swirling, shimmering solar wind activity.

There was that, of course – plus Scorpius-Centaurus was the casino capital of the galaxy. What better place to build a multitude of massive, high-stake, high-class casinos and resorts than throughout one of the top ten natural galactic wonders.

The stakes were high at Scorpius-Centaurus, fortunes were won and lost, no expense spared, and with all the glitz and glamour it was definitely one of those places where anyone who was anyone had to be seen.

Then there were the tourist spots that hosted casino and star tours, of which the 18 to 35s Grand Galaxy Getaway tours apparently took 60 mega-sentrons to complete. We say 'apparently' because the first tour hadn't actually returned yet. And of course the souvenir stands did a roaring trade in 5D imagisers, exploding star globes and 'Why I Survived the Perseus Black Hole Bungee Jump' T-shirts.

Staying at one of the many luxury hotels could literally be a once-in-a-lifetime experience. Hotel star ratings were forever on the move. Forget 5-star, according to the latest tourist industry information, hotel specifications were up to 10-star rating and climbing. The situation was getting so competitive that anything less than the best was considered a has-been and was quickly demolished to make way for the next generation of super-luxury. So quickly, in fact, that guest checkout was often overlooked when it came to hotel upgrade. All part of the fun of the Scorpius-Centaurus casino circuit, complete with that awesome galactic lightshow backdrop.

IQ couldn't have cared less about any of this, however. The magnificent spacescape passed him by unnoticed. He knew that one thing you wouldn't find throughout Scorpius-Centaurus region was a rare type of antigravite ore known as Y2K. And it was Y2K he needed to power his spaceship.

Slouched in his seat, eyes half closed, cigarette in one hand, tapping the console with the other, he wearily gazed at the controls. The fuel gauge needle was on E. He glared at it. The gauge's bowser-shaped fluoro-green display emanated a look of smugness, as if saying to him, 'Told you so!'

IQ let out a lazy groan.

He'd been running on empty for several ship-days, and in order to conserve what little fuel was left, he'd instructed his navigation computer, navcom, to switch to the frightful eco-mode and carry out as many suborbital slingshot manoeuvres as was practical. At this slow speed, he dreaded to think how long it would take getting from A to B.

Setting off from A was the easy bit, mainly because he'd already done it. It was his home planet, Sirius C Major. And for a while he streaked across the great void at a fairly respectable pace of several times the speed of light, occasionally blitzing the odd stray microquasar jet stream along the way. Destination B was Fleurius 12, the twelfth planet in the Fleurius system, some 3.5 light-years away. At least, that was the plan. Unfortunately, due to the fickle nature of space-time, plans tend to change.

IQ was a rev 3; a proud race, descendent from the rev 2.1s of the numerical format era. Rev, of course, meaning 'revision'. The various revision populations were spread across the three planets orbiting Sirius C. IQ's home planet, C Major, was the middle one – easily the best looking of the bunch, being spherical.

IQ's job was a freelance gofer. His current mission was to boldly set out and find a star translayer for a large research company based on Crux Alumina, a planet in the nearby Acrux system. A star translayer is a specialised piece of equipment, made from specialised materials unavailable within the Sirius or Acrux systems. IQ didn't know too much about what a star translayer was or what it was required for, but his ship's navcom did, which was appropriate, as it was the sort of thing navcoms were supposed to know.

The original plan was to borrow one from The Great Fleurius University on Fleurius 12. Fleurius 12 also used to be a well-known Y2K fuel stop for travellers skirting the upper perimeter of the Ursa Major Nebula, but all Y2K mining had stopped due to environmental pressures from the Save The Wormhole Group.

The story goes, one of the larger mines was encroaching on the site of a mythical space-time wormhole, believed to have been instrumental in transporting ancestors through space and time from Fleurius 12 to Fleurius 14, thus avoiding Fleurius 13 which was considered unlucky.

An interesting tale, but hard to prove, considering Fleurius 14 doesn't actually exist in the real universe and Fleurius 13 doesn't exist at all. But the environmentalists won the day, and ten thousand robo-excavators were put out of work, and the longest resource consent appeal case in the known universe commenced.

At the last official update of the case, Fleurius council representatives were into their fifth generation and the STW Group were arguing amongst themselves about how they were going to spend their latest lot of government grants.

IQ wasn't particularly interested in any of this when he was enquiring about the translayer, but it turned out to be the lead-up story to what had happened to it. Apparently, a student had mistaken it for a wormhole-measuring device and had it sent to Fleurius 13. Needless to say, it hadn't been seen since. But IQ was told where he could get another. Unfortunately, it was a long way away.

The other unfortunate thing was that Y2K, as an energy source, was rapidly becoming obsolete. The mining strike had gone on for so long that everyone thought it would be a lot easier just to update the energy technology. So a new energy source, synthlight, had recently been developed and was considered the next big thing in interstellar travel.

IQ was now living on hope. Y2K was no longer available within the Fleurius system and no one could direct him to the next fuel stop. The worst thing, he supposed, was that he would just have to trade his ship in for a later model at some point. But things were not that desperate just yet. IQ might have been suffering a certain amount of frustration, bordering on mental illness, but he was not suicidal, at least not yet, and he was not going to let go of his beloved ship lightly.

Despite IQ's apparent indifference towards most things, he was actually very fond of his spaceship. It was a 77 Dodge Star. Built in a bygone era when they used real geo-metal and not so much hydrocarbonate copolymers. It had a huge Z80 engine with interstellar overdrive and megatron afterburners. The body was the more retro-looking Mk I with over-flared fins and lots of chrome and all the geo-metal finished in high-gloss candy-apple red.

It was a fairly small ship by modern standards, designed to carry a maximum of six, but IQ had never been particularly fussed on crew or passengers. His ship was pristine, mint, in brand-new condition, inside and out, and he wanted to keep it that way. A very tidy classic, but running on empty. And as the ship gradually slowed down to conserve fuel, the journey was becoming extremely dull. Even the navcom was finding other ways to pass the time and kept pestering IQ for a game of 5D snakes and supersonic elevators.

Space travel is pretty straightforward if you want to go slow. You just push yourself off and, due to the lack of friction, you just keep going. You can go on forever if you want and die of old age before you reach the next celestial body. However, if you want to go fast, it requires a bit of cleverness.

There are various means of going fast, depending on how fast you want to go and how much you want to spend. IQ's ship could go many times the speed of light on a good day. The on-board Z80 engine completely ignored any laws of quantum physics and generated a linear gravitational singularity a few milliseconds into the future, which effectively sucked the spaceship forward – a bit like the donkey and the carrot principle. The theory goes, the donkey hurtles along at such a rate its existence becomes blurred as its time reference is altered, and it begins to not exist very well.

While this sounds a bit uncomfortable for the donkey, it suffered no ill effects, as its time and space references were moving with it. It could have been standing still, for all it knew. And that was the great achievement in gravitational singularity propulsion research – no donkeys were harmed in its development. With no gravitational singularity being generated, the spaceship would slow down to the speed of light, which could be highly inconvenient.

Hurtling through space many times the speed of light is all very well, but it does have its problems, namely steering. Trouble is, things come at you very fast; too fast for the more pedestrian speeds of normal light being emitted and reflected off things to be seen. You will hit it before you see it.

The key to not hitting anything is to know where everything is and just avoid it. This is partially done by navigation computers being very smart things indeed and continuously updating themselves.

When dealing with the whole infinite thing, the process of getting from A to B throughout the universe is broken down to the simple principle of, 'Let's take this one step at a time, shall we?', and navigation computers pride themselves on getting their respective spaceships to the next planet before the crew have pushed the go button.

But in order to cross vast interstellar distances, no one, not even navigation computers, wants to contemplate the huge distances involved – they're just too huge. Better to navigate the journey in a series of short hops; that way, everybody thinks they're achieving something. It also makes it a lot easier to avoid hitting things along the way. Particularly when at least one of the things is moving very fast.

The rest is down to pure luck.

At the speed his ship was currently going, neither IQ nor his navcom was particularly concerned about hitting anything. As far as IQ was concerned, they were travelling frustratingly slowly and at that rate he'd never complete his mission. As far as the navcom was concerned, at that speed it could navigate and steer within a billionth of its maximum processing power.

Fortunately, revs are particularly suited to space travel. In fact, they're routinely hired to carry out long-duration space missions by neighbouring races, as well as their own kind. The thing is, revs don't like company and would much prefer spending vast amounts of time sitting around doing nothing by themselves than having to stew over the irritating habits of anyone else. Of course, they get impatient and stressed that it's taking so long, but they cope with it by using another of their well-developed traits – laziness.

Another thing revs are good at, and this probably explains their preference for solitude (we say 'probably' because trying to get any deep and meaningful sentiments out of a rev has meant that all rev behavioural studies have been based on guesswork) is telepathy. And the downside of telepathy is that you have no secrets; neither does anyone else in the vicinity.

However, the useful thing about telepathy is that it is a very convenient interface to navcoms and the like. So IQ could quite happily televerse with the ship's navcom and receive any data it cared to send his way.

Just to break the monotony, IQ scanned the console once again for any sign that things might get exciting. His eyes rested on the ship's journey clock. It told him he was 6,250 sentrons into his trip. This he already knew. Even though he had no reassuring time references, like convenient sunrises and sunsets, his telepathic abilities meant that, when he felt like it, he was in sync with the ship's navcom.

However, like most revs, he had somewhat selective tele-sync. His navcom had so much processing power that things could get rather out of hand if he tried to keep up with it. He merely dipped in and out of its data stream on occasion or would simply ignore it and ask questions later.

IQ's concentration returned slightly to what was going on, which appeared to be precisely nothing. He propped his elbow on the window ledge and gazed through the quarter-light to check his wing mirror. He fiddled with the wing mirror joystick – nothing happening there, he thought.

He gazed out towards the infinitely majestic dust clouds of Upper Perseus, several light-years away, yet seemingly tantalisingly close. He didn't give two hoots about the vastness of the cloud formations and the fact that they consisted of a billion stars, a billion planets and that the 18 to 35s Grand Galaxy Getaway tours were out there somewhere, evidently having a good time. He didn't think about the overwhelmingly stunning colour changes that seemed to evolve through each other. And he couldn't have cared less about the upper outer fringes radiating high-energy cosmic rays of bright reds, moody greens and indifferent shades of magenta, reaching right across to Orion Spur.

He focused on the control console once more, reached out and tapped the fuel gauge in the vain hope it was an instrument error. The needle dropped into the red, and cigarette ash dropped into his drink. He let out a long, loud, weary groan.

Chapter 2

"All right, good afternoon everybody and welcome to Audio Electronics stage three. No one in the wrong class? Excellent. My name is Rick Wakefield, and I'll be taking you through the next six weeks on this fascinating subject where we explore the intricacies of sound processing. My background is in the power amp industry and ..."

"Isn't he the keyboardist in Yes?" George whispered to Steve.

Steve glanced sideways at George and shrugged.

Rick Wakefield continued, "And I manage the audio electronics lab. Perhaps you'd like to introduce yourself?" Rick asked George.

"Who me?" George said, all innocent-like.

"Yes, you."

"How?"

"The usual way," Rick suggested.

"Ah, George Haley."

"Know much about audio electronics, George?" Rick asked.

"A little bit," George replied.

"Which bit is that exactly?"

George quickly gathered his thoughts. “Oh, well, I’m putting together an app to control PA sound parameters. It’s my final year project.”

“OK, that sounds like fun. You using the E-jet platform?”

George nodded. E-jet was the standard app tool for year three.

“Right,” said Rick thoughtfully. “It would be more computer programming than electronic hardware, though, wouldn’t it?”

George nodded again, wondering where this conversation was heading.

“So, as I said before, are you in the right class?”

“Yes,” George said, relieved that it was an easy question to answer. “I have to work on my interfacing.”

“Ah, interfacing,” Rick said with relish. “Anyone else doing app programming?” A few hands were raised. “Well, I’ve got some good news. We’ll be going over device interfacing later in the course, including IR, Wi-Fi, Bluetooth and USB ...”

George was in his third year at the Auckland University, studying electronics and computer science. This year’s project was a live sound mixing software app which he was in the process of field testing and he had sensibly named SoundLive. It was a sound management system which enabled real-time live sound mixing of bands for both a real and online audience.

He’d actually started developing the app the year before, so he had a good head start, and as well as looking to be a winning project, he felt it also had commercial possibilities.

He was also a bit of a muso. One of the first things he bought, once he got a student loan, was a synthesiser – a second-hand Korg Wavestation. He taught himself to play and was in various bands during his first couple of years at uni, but all the while, he tinkered with sound-related software.

George would probably describe himself as witty, fairly intelligent, empathetic, and maybe a bit quirky. But everyone else thought him odd. Probably his greatest strength was perseverance with things he was passionate about, which unfortunately did not include his studies.

He was twenty, a skinny white geek, generally quiet with a harmless but serious demeanour. Most people meeting him for the first time would think he appeared considerate and charming in a shy sort of way, until he did or said something, and then they would just think him odd.

He had a sarcastic streak, and his witty moments usually consisted of dry one-liners that not everyone necessarily got. Hence the Rick Wakefield comment, which had gone completely over Steve's head.

George was also a bit of a space nut – although he'd prefer to keep this to himself, as he thought it might be perceived as being a bit too geeky. But he was secretly obsessed with all things NASA. In fact, he wanted to be an astronaut at one stage but eventually settled on building a scale model of the space shuttle instead, which gradually fell into disrepair as it was further modified with extra lights, servo motors and laser cannons. One small step, as they say.

Sitting next to him in class was his friend Steve. Steve played bass for a local band Dark City and had completed a diploma in audio engineering. Like George, he decided to do the audio electronics course to better understand the sound gear he frequently used in his start-up business. He ran his own events management company and his next planned event was a gig in the university's main courtyard.

He was hoping to feature a few local bands including his own.

Steve wasn't a geek, or at least didn't particularly look like one. He was a relaxed and friendly guy, with a dark complexion, dark curly hair, and an air of streetwise coolness about him. He loved his music, particularly hard rock and metal that his band often thrashed out with vigour.

George and Steve had met in first year and both had been in and out of various bands ever since. George wasn't really a full-time member of Dark City; he just played keyboards for them on the odd occasion, as he spent most of his time developing SoundLive.

Towards the end of Rick's course introduction, the session was interrupted with yet another ground tremor.

"Wasn't me," Steve reassuringly announced.

The tremors had been occurring for the last week and were very much confined to the university area. Although they were classified as tremors, they were more like bursts of low-frequency hums coming from the ground. Geologists and city officials had been on the news all week offering their theories and assurances. They weren't classified as earthquakes, and a volcano was definitely ruled out, but there was reasonable certainty the tremors were natural. What they failed to realise was that the tremors had started immediately after a new substation had been installed in the main university block.

"OK, maybe that's a good time to take a break," Rick said. "Just before we do, I'll quickly introduce you to our resident recording studio engineer, Scotty."

A stocky, mid-height, long-straggly-ginger-haired, checked-flannel-shirt-wearing Scotsman leapt up from the front row. "Thank ye, Rick, ma mun," Scotty announced. "Ma naim eh Scotty. Ye cun call meh Scotty, but. Aw kae?

Ahm eh awdiaw engineer. Seh?" he said proudly. "Ah ivin pronownced thaht reet. No, eff ye wan tae boack th stawdiaw, ye comb an seh meh, aw kae? Heers a wee info fer ye. Grahb em as ye goh oat. Reet, awac wi ye."

The class was looking fairly stunned at this point.

Luckily, Rick moved things along. "While you're all thinking about that, we'll have a break. Back here quarter to three."

As they filed out, George and Scotty nodded at each other.

"Seh ye laeter, Georgie," Scotty said.

"Yep, sure."

George and Steve headed for the student café.

"Yeah," George said to Steve, "the lecturer, Rick Wakefield. He's the keyboard player in Yes."

"What's Yes?" Steve asked, out of politeness rather than genuine interest.

"Prog rock band."

"Ah well, there you go, you see," Steve replied. "Prog rock went out fifty years ago and now he has to teach to make a living. He should be doing some speed metal or hard funk."

"You should suggest that to him," George said.

They got their usual drinks – a coffee for George and a Coke for Steve – and sat at their usual table.

"Good to see Scotty again," Steve said. "Even if I can never understand him."

"I can understand him OK."

Steve laughed. "I think you're the only one who can. You seeing him later?"

"Yeah, just to talk about SoundLive," George said. He then changed the subject. "So this gig you're organising – how many bands are playing?"

"At this stage, four. All uni bands."

"OK."

"Seconds To Go, a three-piece, simple pop-type thing. You seen them?" Steve asked.

"No. Has anybody?"

"Oh yeah. They're playing at the Space Cadet tomorrow night. And Lazy Brain and Foulmouth maybe, and us."

George was hoping to use the gig to do some tests on SoundLive in a real environment. "Yep. Who's doing the PA?"

"It's the student union's," Steve explained. "We're putting it all together ourselves. They use the same set-up in the courtyard all the time. It's a digital desk. So you'll be able to tap into that with your box of tricks. It's pretty relaxed, really. No biggie."

"Right," George replied, deep in thought.

If George was impressed with Steve's event managing, he didn't show it. He had only done one live test of his software and that was in the student bar with Steve's band. It went well, but later he had to work on the equalization and reduce latency on the analogue-to-digital converter. He was quietly confident that with Scotty's help he'd have it all together by the courtyard gig.

"Fancy a smoke?" Steve asked, preparing to stand. The café and courtyard were no smoking zones, so their choices were the smoking zone at the back of the main block, or the reserve, on the other side of the boundary fence.

"OK," George replied as he pushed his chair back. Even though he wasn't a smoker, he occasionally indulged in the odd reefer, spliff or joint that Steve always seemed to produce with ease.

They both went outside carrying their drinks and made their way down the path to the reserve to find a discreet smoking place. The reserve was a wide belt of native bush that separated the university's playing fields from the city cemetery. It was a sanctuary for several native bird species and numerous homeless derelicts. The underside of the motorway overbridge that ran over the far end of the reserve provided cover for an assortment of improvised digs for the homeless characters, which half the city's pigeons shat all over.

George and Steve positioned themselves discreetly at a bend in the path on the edge of the reserve about midway between the university and the motorway, so they could easily see anyone approaching from any direction. Not that they were worried about getting caught smoking dope, it's just that it gives the impression of being more cool if you look as if you're being discreet. If you're too discreet, nobody will notice how cool you are, so that's a waste of time. You want to be discreet yet be noticed so people think you've got a good reason to be discreet and therefore you must be very cool indeed.

"Only got a couple of minutes," said Steve as he passed the joint to George. He then handed over a small bag of cannabis. "Here, try this later, when you're in the mood."

"Oh great," said George. "I was after some more parsley." He put it in his satchel.

"It's got sage, rosemary and thyme in it as well."

"Excellent. I'll make a salad," George joked. "So how's the City going?"

"Good. Looking forward to the Summer Sizzler gig," said Steve, taking the joint back.

"Cool. I'll be there," said George.

He noticed one of the homeless characters further down the path looking at them. "I'm supposed to be helping out on the main stage. Probably monitors. We got an all-up meeting about it tomorrow night." He took another drag. The guy was slowly shuffling towards them.

"Great," Steve replied. "You can give *us* a good monitor mix and all the other bands a shit one," he laughed.

"I'm gonna take SoundLive with me," said George. "Scotty's helped me set up a demo for some industry guys. I'm talking to him about it later. You can tag along if you like."

"When you say 'talk to Scotty', I take it you mean in the broadest sense," said Steve.

The homeless guy was getting closer. Oh Christ, thought George, why do morons always come up to you? It's always the same. If you're walking down the street with a sense of purpose, no one bothers you. But as soon as you stop – maybe you're waiting for someone or looking at something – straight away you're a magnet for all sorts of weirdos and scroungers.

Steve continued, "Sure, I'll tag along in support. Might learn something."

"Like how to understand Scottish in three easy lessons," George suggested.

Steve laughed. "It's not his Scottish I'm worried about, it's his English."

They were both aware of the encroaching figure, and sure enough, the character stopped right in front of them, a look of concern on his face.

"What's up, bro?" Steve asked with a spaced-out grin. There was no immediate response. He murmured to George, "I think he's more out of it than we are."

"No, we haven't got any money. Go away," said George, rather irritated.

"It's coming again," the old guy said suddenly, darting his eyes left and right.

"That's nice," Steve said. "What's coming?"

"It's coming here. Yes," the guy said, nodding. "From space, don't you know." He glanced down the path, looking suitably spooked.

"Great," said George. "We'll look forward to it."

The old guy stared wide-eyed at George. He then suddenly looked up and pointed at the sky. He dropped his face to stare at George again. George burst out laughing, which set Steve off.

The homeless guy was maybe early-to-mid fifties, with a mess of dark-grey hair all round his face and sticking out from under his woolly hat. He wore several layers of clothing, complete with a huge trench coat and sneakers with untied laces sticking out from underneath. Strange thing was he had impeccable teeth that seemed to radiate from the jumbled shambles of the rest of him.

He suddenly smiled at George. "Oh, I am sorry. Do beg your pardon. Have a good afternoon," he said, raising his bottle, bowing slightly and then walking on.

George and Steve were taken aback by his sudden change in demeanour. They watched him amble down the path. He certainly wasn't walking in a straight line, and George figured he'd easily walk twice the distance than his chosen route.

"Well," George said. "There's a bit of useless information for you."

"What's that?"

George pulled a demented face and gibbered, "It's coming. From out of space."

"Oh, that. Here," Steve said, offering George a stick of gum.

"Ta." George shoved it in his mouth. "So what do you think is coming again?"

"Ah, let's see, Christmas? Your first shag?"

"What?" George demanded, slightly defensively.

They wandered back into class as Rick Wakefield was kicking off the second half with intricacies of class AB amplifiers. They were still buzzing, but neither had any concern about whether they were in a suitable state to concentrate, be able to write things down or were even looking particularly attentive. The second half of a three-hour afternoon lecture was always a chore, whether you were awake or not – everyone knew it; it was to be expected. So their doped-out expression would more than likely go unnoticed.

George started thinking about what the homeless guy was trying to say. He'd said: 'It's coming from space.' Probably the usual rambling nonsense that homeless people seemed to have a knack for. The guy certainly said it with conviction, though, George would give him that.

"George?" Rick Wakefield called out.

The sound of Rick's voice echoed around in George's brain as he struggled to snap back to reality.

"What?" he finally said.

"Isn't that right, George?" Rick asked.

"Oh ... ah ... yeah ..." George replied, hoping that was enough.

"PA power amps are a good example of class AB amplification. Would you agree, being the all-round expert on such things?"

"Yes," said George, nodding. "Absolutely."

Steve sniggered under his breath.

There were a few more ground tremors during the remainder of the lecture. Each time, students seemed to look up as if they might spot it coming from the ceiling.

The lecture finally concluded, and George and Steve filed out into the corridor and made their way to the café. Steve could sense a growing excitement ready to burst out of George.

Sure enough ...

"I have a theory," George said with great enthusiasm.

"Oh God, here it comes."

"You know the university's built on a volcano field, right?"

"That's your theory, is it? It's brilliant. Simple and to the point," Steve said, hoping that was it.

"Wait, there's more to it."

"I'm sure there is."

"The ancient lava fields have lava caves, right?"

"If you say so."

"And you know the tremors began right after they installed that substation in the main block, right?"

"Right," Steve replied.

"Well, I reckon the 50-hertz hum from the transformer is resonating with a lava cave under the university," George said proudly.

There was a bit of a pause before Steve added, "A slight flaw in your theory. The hum from a transformer is constant. This tremor hum is intermittent."

"Yes, but many different variables create resonance," George explained. "Load, temperature, weather ..."

"Weather?" Steve questioned, doubtfully.

"Of course. When it rains, it partly fills the lava cave with water, changing its resonance properties. Didn't it rain yesterday?"

"No."

"Well, the day before then."

"No, it hasn't rained all week," Steve pointed out.

"No, well, it could have," George said in partial defeat. He persevered. "But that's not my point. Ah, what is my point?"

"Fucked if I know," Steve guffawed.

"I mean, that's just one variable, you see."

"What is?"

"The rain." George looked highly pleased with himself.

Bewildered, Steve shook his head. "Yeah, I got a theory," he said. "This is a good one, you'll like this."

"What's that?"

"Let's go to the pub."

George considered this favourably; on the merits it seemed fairly achievable. "Yeah, OK."

"What time are we seeing Scotty?" Steve asked.

"Six."

"Right, we've got half an hour."

The local student pub, The Space Cadet, was situated just across the road and, conveniently, happy hour was between five and six.

"Now we'll have no more talk about humming lava caves, OK?" Steve said as they entered.

George put on a determined look. "The pitfalls of urban living," he stressed, as if it were obvious.

Steve gave him a puzzled glance then decided against prolonging the agony. Alcohol had priority. And he made a beeline for the bar.

IQ suddenly sat up. No, that didn't help. His eyes scanned the cabin. It looked reassuringly familiar. He asked the navcom if cabin's enviro-reality feature was active. It wasn't; his surroundings were real.

Satisfied, he slouched back down in his seat and gazed out his port-side window. Absolutely nothing as far as the eye could see. Other than all those billions of stars out there, looking curiously blurred. Just imagine, he thought, on one of those stars is what I'm looking for.

Suddenly he realised what was different – the ship was travelling astoundingly fast. He scanned the controls. Eco-mode was still activated, but the speed was well into the red.

What's this? IQ televersed the navcom. *Another black hole?*

Kind of, the navcom replied. *We're hitching a ride on the Scorpius-Centaurus super space-time network.*

This was a handy little feature of the region specifically designed to whizz punters and tourists around the various casino joints and attraction mega-centres. You enter the network through a convenient stellar black hole which then takes you to any number of space-time wormholes that transport you around different parts of the vast Scorpius-Centaurus wonderland at breakneck speed.

They were expected to jump out of the network at the outer reaches of Orion's Arm very soon. The navcom then asked for no interruptions while it calculated the correct exit angle so they could freewheel in a straight line to the end of Orion Spur without hitting anything along the way.

Fine, whatever, IQ responded, as he tapped the end of a cigarette on the console. Then, intrigued, he asked, *Why Orion Spur?*

This will take us to the Sagittarius Arm, the navcom responded.

Fine, whatever. IQ lit the cigarette and blew smoke at the ceiling. He gazed around the console. He pressed a button that he liked the look of. Then he asked, *What's a Sagittarius?*

Shush! came the short, sharp response.

Fine, IQ replied glumly. He slid off his seat and headed for the galley. This consisted of a few small panels in the rear wall of the flight deck. He pressed the lunch button. There was a slight whirr-click sound and one of the panels slid open revealing his lunch. He took the package back to his seat, unwrapped it and began munching on something that looked suspiciously like a cream doughnut.

We're coming up on the exit point, the navcom informed him. *Real space-time should then continue as before, and with any luck you should be the same age as when you entered.*

IQ already knew these network systems were constructed using liberal amounts of dark space which effectively countered the annoying and potentially embarrassing time-dilation effects commonly associated with getting too involved in special relativity phenomena.

The navcom then advised that he buckle up as there might be a few bumps on exit. IQ did as he was told, and sure enough, there was a sudden tremendous amount of G-force as the ship careered through the space-time curve and back into real space. He had the alarming feeling that his body desperately wanted to shoot up and hit the ceiling very hard. He let out a short, indecipherable exclamation.

He'd only experienced a manoeuvre like this once before. When he first bought his ship, he took it out for a run to see what it was capable of. He'd switched the controls to manual and headed out of the Sirius system so he could really open it up. He was going flat out and feeling rather pleased with himself when the navcom casually asked him if he'd rather not hit anything. Because if he didn't, the miss-everything mode would have to be activated pretty damn soon.

IQ was madly pressing buttons and flipping switches, and his reply was to the effect of, *Yeah baby, let's move this mother!*

The navcom took this as an affirmative and slammed the ship into a negative-singularity power dive, effectively borrowing all the gravitational energy from the planet it was about to hit to divert their path enough to avoid anything nasty.

That time, IQ did indeed hit the ceiling. After he came to, he had a frank discussion with the navcom, and they eventually came to an amicable understanding of how things were going to go in future. And from then on, IQ always allowed the navcom to have at least some means of automatic control.

Automatic control was preferable anyway, especially on long space flights where the miss-everything mode was pretty much essential.

IQ gazed around the cabin as he was gathering his thoughts back to what he was doing before he was interrupted with that rather dramatic out-of-body experience. He unbuckled his belt and did a bit of a stretch. As he flexed his neck back he couldn't help notice the remains of a cream doughnut splattered across the ceiling.

George and Steve were propped up at a bar table, not talking about lava caves.

"Hey, there's that homeless fella," Steve said, eyeing the pub entrance.

"Oh yeah," George said. "I've never seen him in here before. Have you?"

"No. But then, I've never looked out for him."

"Hmm," said George thoughtfully. "Probably the sort you'd take no notice of."

"Stands out now, though."

George laughed. "Yeah, he does. Maybe he's a student."

"Maybe he's a lecturer. One of those professor fellas."

"Right, yes," George replied in agreement and feeling another round of pointless pub banter coming on. "Based on what he told us earlier, I'd go to his lectures."

"Absolutely," Steve replied. "Maybe learn some social psychology ... a bit of rocket science, perhaps."

"Of course! He must be an astrophysicist. I mean, he knows his stuff, doesn't he? Things coming from space and that."

"Definitely. He's probably from space himself," Steve suggested.

George laughed. "Well, you never know who's among

us, eh. Are we all human from planet Earth?"

"Looks like he's got a mate."

"One of his alien mates."

The old guy was talking to another punter who had bought him, of all things, a cup of tea.

"Well he's a local," George said. A sudden thought occurred to him. "I wonder what his theories are on the ground tremors."

"I'm sure you two would have a right old chat about that," Steve replied. "Bloody hell. It'd be like the big conspiracy discussion of the century."

George chuckled. "I don't really think of myself as a conspiracist."

"Nah, mate, you're a natural-born rocket scientist. Speaking of which, do we need to get going?"

George looked at his phone. "Yep. Let's go see the mad Scotsman."

They finished their drinks and got ready to leave.

"Looks like your mate's gone," Steve said, nodding in the direction where the old guy had been.

"He'll be lecturing a night class, I expect."

They exited onto the street and began walking back towards the university gates.

"There he is," George said, pointing up the road.

The old guy was standing in the middle of the footpath staring up at the evening sky.

"I think you're right," Steve said. "He's an astrophysicist."

Chapter 3

IQ sat bolt upright with a Y2K alarm going off in his head. His navcom had detected Y2K, not too far away. Or at least not too far away relative to the light-year distances of open space. It was actually off the screen, so it would still take a while to get there. Finally things were getting exciting.

Although it was slightly off IQ's planned route, he instructed the navcom to make a beeline for it. The navcom said they'd be able to change course at the next suborbital slingshot manoeuvre, about 1,000 sentrons from now, give or take.

IQ sank back in his seat.

Where is it?

Somewhere on the outer reaches of the Orion Spur, near the Orion Nebula.

Doesn't ring any bells, IQ replied.

Hopefully it was just one of those many insignificant, random collections of floating rocks that no one had discovered yet, he thought. And he'd be able to steam in without making a scene, grab a bunch of Y2K to last a lifetime and be on his way in a jiffy. Little did IQ know that his hopes were really quite high indeed.

IQ's preference was to avoid bumping into anyone during his missions. Especially someone he knew. The chances of this occurring in the vastness of outer space were usually very slim, but it happened more often than he was comfortable with. Not literally bumping into someone, as such, but navcoms, being very clever devices, would often communicate with other navcoms in spaceships near or far. And as soon as that happened, you'd effectively bumped into someone.

And you never knew who you might meet. You may have been crossing vast interstellar distances for ages, out in the middle of nowhere, maybe even half-dosed up on cryonics, and suddenly you had to deal with the awkwardness of being sociable. IQ had often had to take evasive action just to avoid the sort of embarrassment that tended to occur at such events.

Well, not so much embarrassment, more like irritation. Especially if they're driving a whizzier spaceship than yours. It was only embarrassing when you couldn't remember their name, especially right after your navcom had just told you. Fortunately, this wasn't a common occurrence, because being telepathic, IQ would only forget someone's name if they'd forgotten it themselves. And when subjected to the agonisingly vast durations of space travel, there were some who did indeed forget their own names.

This unfortunate affliction highlighted another attribute that revs were good at and made them ideal for long space flights; they were immune to STFS, or, Space Travel Forgetfulness Syndrome. Not a lot is known about this problem, other than it exists, because those who were assigned to carry out the necessary data-gathering exercises for STFS study usually forgot what they went out for in the first place. You wouldn't catch a rev carrying out such a survey, however. Although they were good at remembering things like their own name, they did consider certain tasks beneath them. Especially when it involved beings with whizzier spaceships.

Despite all this, however, IQ's mood was lifting. And as the cosmic rays radiating from the upper outer fringes of Orion Spur turned from deep red to majestic magenta, IQ felt pleasantly optimistic. *Is it likely we'll find a star translayer in this neck of the woods?* he enquired.

After a slight pause, the navcom reported, *I seem to be receiving a translayer signal that appears to be coming from the outer end of Orion Spur, the Solar System, to be precise.*

IQ would have raised one eyebrow if he'd had any. *Really? Never heard of it.* He lit up a cigarette, took a deep drag and blew smoke at the ceiling. *Let me know when you find out more*, he asked.

Hang on, the navcom replied.

After a moment it confirmed star translayer activity. *There seems to be multiple units.*

IQ didn't raise both eyebrows. *Multiple? Really? Have we hit the jackpot?* Knowing that star translayers are a fairly rare thing – as far as he knew – he then asked the obvious question. *Why would there be multiple?*

Because it appears that's where they make them, the navcom replied.

IQ slumped in his seat as he thought about this. If this all turns out to be true, he really has hit the jackpot. Maybe he could change his business; be a star translayer importer. He'd be the exclusive agent in the Sirius system.

But it would need a careful approach. If that's where translayers are made, he thought, there must be a sizable population in the region. Logic would suggest that if any population was intelligent enough to make translayers, they must have discovered the merits of using Y2K, surely?

And if that's the case, it should be relatively easy to get hold of. If they've discovered it, that is. Hopefully it's not buried in a prehistoric swamp or something equally inconvenient.

He waited for the navcom to update. *Well?* he asked, impatiently.

Well what?

What sort of population are we dealing with? Are they using Y2K? And just how intelligent are they? And who do they sell their translayers to? Is there an exclusive market?

Still working on it, came the reply.

IQ took another drag on his cigarette and gazed out at the multicoloured cosmic display of Orion Nebula. Despite the obvious benefits, he normally found habitable zones to be quite annoying. The trouble was they invariably attracted all sorts of odd lifeforms that you had to deal with in one way or another. And it was the intelligent ones that were the most annoying. Worse still if they hadn't made interstellar contact yet. In that case he'd really have to tread carefully.

The navcom interrupted his train of thought. *Brace yourself*, it advised, *here comes a whole stream of data about the planet Earth.*

Chapter 4

Several days later, on a bright, sunny morning, George was approaching the entrance to the university's main block when he noticed a barricaded-off area on one side of the courtyard. It looked something like roadworks, though obviously not on the road; therefore, George thought, it must be just works.

A few students were standing around the perimeter looking at what was inside, so George stopped to have a look himself. The barricaded area was about 10 metres in diameter and had a couple of men-at-work signs in strategic places. Right in the centre of the work zone was a rock sticking partway out of the ground. Any non-rock enthusiast would regard it as a fairly big rock. But in fact it was fairly small. Or at least it was small considering what it was doing.

George had a feeling there was something special about this rock, as did most people when they approached it. It was almost as if it radiated some invisible energy that heightened your senses. People seemed to like standing there looking at it, like a circle of cold, homeless people warming themselves around a brazier.

The rock itself was sticking roughly a metre out of the

shallow pit that had been dug around it. It was larger in the middle, roughly half a metre in diameter, tapering off at each end, although one end was below ground. It looked very heavy. Aside from its apparent radiant power, the other thing that intrigued everyone was its colour. It was jet black, or maybe very dark blue, with a translucent quality. Very glossy, quite shiny and new-looking, and hard as a diamond, as it turned out. Certainly nothing like the usual volcanic-based rock normally found around the city.

Needless to say, the university's geology department was going nuts over it. Lead by Dr Brian Segway, a full-time lecturer and research director, specialising in geology, mineralogy and volcanology, a select team of students were buzzing around the rock carrying out all sorts of tests and gathering data.

They also had a small team with a metal detector going around the grounds looking for signs of any more strange rocks. They managed to detect many things, including a high-voltage electricity supply cable, some footpath reinforcing and various water pipes. Thankfully they didn't try and dig these things up, but there was one moment that caused excitement when they unearthed a rusted steering wheel from the begonia bed. Dr Segway reeled the students in before they set about looking for the rest of the car.

Second-year student Charlene Dibble, usually known as Charley, was part of the geology team. On this particular day, it was her job to determine the hardness of the rock using a sclerometer and to take a number of small samples for lab analysis. It was this latter task that was causing her grief; the rock just refused to chip.

She was all decked out with safety glasses, gloves, hard hat and white disposable overalls, and had slowly gone through some of the more delicate rock chipping instruments and was about to lay into the thing with a hammer and chisel.

Meanwhile, George stood at the worksite barrier for a couple of minutes looking in and looking suitably vacant, just like all the other half-mesmerised idiots watching on.

In fact, he and Charley had had eyes on each other for a while now. But with all her get-up, he didn't recognise her. He was about to call out to her to be careful with that or she might have someone's eye out, or some smart-arse comment like that, when his pathetic train of thought was interrupted.

"Hiya, Georgie boy." A thick Scottish accent greeted George. "Waa we goh here thun?"

"Oh, hi Scotty. I dunno. Weird-looking rock."

"Aye, ah cun seh thaht. Hello, darlin'," he called to Charley.

She looked up, saw George and smiled at him. George half-smiled back, a little perplexed that the girl had acknowledged him. Scotty, of course, thought she was smiling at him. "Ye wan tae be carefaw wi tha thung," he said to her. "Ye halve some woan's ah oat."

Charley smiled, put the tools down and picked up a hammer drill.

"Hey, I was hoping to catch up with you later," George said to Scotty. "I'll show you how far I've got with SoundLive."

"Och, aye. Tha sowns gude."

"Yeah, I'm just going ..."

He was interrupted by an almighty clatter from Charley's drilling.

"I'm going up to the computer lab," he yelled in Scotty's ear. "Can we meet up later?"

"Aye. Comb rown tae the stawdiaw aftae lunch, eh?"

George stared at Scotty for a second. "Eh?" he yelled.

"Aftae lunch, boyo," Scotty yelled back.

"Yeah, great, thanks. See you then." George glanced back at Charley, still trying to work out who she was, but she was engrossed in her drilling. He quickly waved at Scotty and moved off.

Later, in the geology lab, Charley was logging on to her geology team's web page to update the day's events. The web page included a description of the rock, which the students had named Black Star, a log of ground tremors, and a few photos. Charley added data collected that day, including photos of the rock and a busted drill, and then sent a link to her long-time friend who was studying nuclear science at San Fernando.

The fragment she'd broken off was small and wedge-shaped with a few ragged edges. It was very dark, but you could see through it, like a dark crystal. She picked it up and studied it under a magnifying glass. She held it up to the light and could see that it was indeed translucent. She turned it slowly in her fingertips and noticed its translucence change as she turned it. She held it steady, but it seemed the translucence was still changing, swirling almost. She turned it back and forth quickly. Inside, it was alive as if it was filled with black smoke. She shook it. The smoke swirled around faster.

"Whoa ..." she whispered, as she watched the mysterious display through the magnifying glass. The swirling gradually slowed down until it was barely moving.

Gobsmacked, she lowered the glass and raised her head to stare at the opposite wall, which, thankfully, wasn't swirling. She focused hers eyes on the fragment again. Does the Black Star do this? she thought. Did anyone notice anything like this today?

She quickly put the fragment back in its cotton-wool-filled vial, pressed the lid on, grabbed her backpack and headed for the door.

Half walking, half running, she hurried towards the excavation site. She stopped briefly at Dr Segway's office and knocked on the door. Barely waiting for an answer she continued on to the site.

She found Dr Segway standing at the side of the pit talking to a couple of workmen who were examining the rock. However, by this time, she was having second thoughts about giving up her tiny piece of Black Star, and she decided not to mention it, for now.

"Hi, Dr Segway," she said.

"Oh, hi Charlene."

"What's happening?" she asked.

"We're trying to work out how to get this up to the lab."

"That'd be good," she said.

"Yes, it'll be a lot easier in a controlled environment. But it's very heavy."

Charley watched the workmen for a second. "Dr Segway?" she asked.

"Mm?"

"Has anyone done any translucence tests on the rock?"

"Nothing useful as yet. Why's that?"

"I think it might be translucent," she said. "But we ran out of time before I could test for that."

"Well, that would make things even more interesting if it is," Dr Segway replied. "Once we get it upstairs, we can test with various light sources."

Charley thought for a second. "Could it be some kind of diamond?"

Dr Segway pondered this. "It's certainly hard enough. We need to determine how it was formed. Whether it's crystal, metamorphic, heat, pressure, those sorts of things."

"It might be valuable," Charley said.

"Oh it is. Undoubtedly."

Charley knew that, technically, her chip of Black Star belonged to the university and she had no intention of keeping it; she was merely studying it. She figured she'd bring it out for the class to inspect at their next lab session. She hadn't put it up on their website just yet, but intended to. However, something made her keep it quiet for now. Once the rock was safely up in the lab, she thought, then she'd share her little piece of Black Star.

IQ woke with a start. Something was wrong. It took him a few seconds to focus his brain on what the navcom was trying to tell him.

Are we there yet? he asked.

Negative. But someone else is making a beeline for the Y2K. They are a lot further from it than we are and coming from another direction, but definitely heading for the same location and definitely a spaceship of some kind.

The navcom wasn't able to give him any more information on the mystery object but promised to work on it.

This is very irritating news, IQ thought. *If the life forms on Earth aren't capable of interstellar travel yet, then who are these guys?* he asked the navcom, *and what are the chances of them detecting us?*

Very likely, came the response, *and we will make contact very soon.*

'Make contact' was a technical term for 'bumping into someone'.

Anyone else out there? IQ asked.

Negative.

IQ didn't like the sound of that. Why would anyone want to go where he was going? We're out in the middle of nowhere, he thought. Scorpius Centaurus is now light-years behind us.

Where exactly are we? he asked.

The region of Orion-Cygnus. Currently entering the outer orbital zones of the Solar System. Earth will be coming up on the screen shortly.

Are they going to see us coming?

Negative. The not-be-seen precautions have been activated.

One of the basic rules of thumb in interstellar travel is never give yourself away on a planet where the inhabitants have never experienced a close encounter. After a quick survey of all the available data, the navcom concluded there was no clear evidence that the current inhabitants of Earth had experienced a close encounter of any kind. Or, if they had, it was not well known. Sure there had been reports of UFOs, particularly following the so called 'Roswell' incident, but it was obvious the planet was divided on the subject. This was enough for the navcom to activate not-be-seen precautions. They needed to lie low and stay out of trouble. Little did they know just how difficult that was going to be.

The ship's not-be-seen system consisted of the light-bending properties of the ship's outer coating and enviro-light-wave sensors that interfaced to the ship's navcom. The whole thing effectively fooled anyone's vision into not seeing the ship. The system even prevented the ship casting a shadow. The navcom could send decoded light-pattern data to IQ telepathically to enable him to see the ship when others couldn't, and IQ could in turn interpret for others telepathically.

And of course it goes without saying that the ship's

radar invisibility made the US B-2 Spirit stealth fighter stick out like a 747 trying to land on the White House lawn. Although IQ had never actually proved this.

IQ could feel the ship slowing down. He buckled his lap belt and pushed his tray table away.

Update on the Y2K, the navcom piped up. *There appears to be only a solitary source. We'll orbit the planet and confirm its location. In the meantime here's a sample of Earth translayer signal.*

A rather grainy and flickery video came up on the monitor screen. It was a TV commercial. A very happy representative from a very happy bank was giving a potential customer a hug, presumably implying this is how good banking works. A happy jingle went along with it, which to IQ's ears, sounded like a cacophony of high-frequency screeches.

Is that them? IQ enquired.

Affirmative.

I don't get it.

You don't have to. This signal is being relayed to translayers on Earth. You just have to locate a receiver.

And I can do that in the vicinity of the Y2K? IQ asked.

We'll soon find out. Initiating pre-orbit tracking. If you look out the port side, you can see the Earth's moon.

IQ gazed out the window for a second. *No atmosphere, huh?*

Affirmative. They have been there, though.

IQ frowned. *Why?*

To get rocks.

IQ nodded. *I can understand that.*

By the time IQ landed on planet Earth, the ship's auxiliary power was dangerously low. It was able to draw solar energy to keep vital circuits running, including the not-be-seen system, but if he was ever going to go anywhere, he would have to get his Y2K.

The navcom found a suitably discreet landing site close to the Y2K. IQ turned the monitor on to panoramic view to survey the area. The ship was parked in a clearing, surrounded by tall vegetation. He noticed an inhabitant of the planet standing on the edge of the clearing, staring at the ship. IQ studied him for a while. *What's this guy looking at?* he asked the navcom.

The navcom was also checking out the individual.

The not-be-seen is activated, isn't it? IQ enquired. In fact, he already knew it was, as he could easily confirm its status through his telepathic link. He was just making sure the navcom was on top of the situation.

At last the navcom responded. *Physical appearance, social status and levels of inebriation indicate the human could say or do anything and other humans would not only not believe him, but completely ignore him. But how he can see the ship is a complete mystery.*

Keep an eye on him, IQ instructed. He then turned his attention to the aerial footage the ship's cameras had captured on the way in. The Y2K position was highlighted on it. It wasn't far from their position, but the area seemed very busy with human activity.

Is it always like this? IQ asked.

The scheduling of local activity suggests that it significantly reduces not long after sunset; in about five hours, the navcom informed.

Scheduling of what?

Lectures.

Chapter 5

Earlier that morning, George woke to a pleasant spring day with the tune of 'Black Star' in his head. He'd had one of those weird dreams where the harder he tried to remember what it was, the more it faded. George had a theory about this – dreams don't reside in memory, he thought, and any recollection you have of them when you wake up is merely the result of residual brainwave energy trying to find a home in your brain. But most dreams are so bizarre they don't fit into a neat category, so they quickly disappear. Although George couldn't remember his dream, he could remember the tune.

He could also remember the title 'Black Star'. He considered the possibility of hypnotising himself to drag out more details about the dream but had his doubts it would be effective; he didn't know how to self-hypnotise, for a start. However, he had a catchy tune and that was enough.

He quickly sprang out of bed, whipped the dust cover off his synthesiser, turned it on, and with a few hastily scrawled lyrics about his theory of dream brainwave energy, wrote 'Black Star'. He then programmed the tune into the synth so he wouldn't forget it.

After a quick breakfast, he gathered his bits together to head off on his mighty Vespa. It was the day of the university gig and he wanted to do some calibration exercises on SoundLive beforehand.

He got to the courtyard and parked his scooter nearby. It didn't seem to matter where he parked it, it never seemed to bother anyone. In fact, that was one of the main reasons he bought it in the first place. People tend to ignore scooters; they're quite happy to walk around them, apparently without any concern or annoyance, possibly because they feel sorry for any rider who voluntarily puts themselves out there to actually be seen on it. Parking wardens don't touch them for fear of risking repercussions of victimising the disabled. Even scooter riders ignore other scooters. The only things that are attracted to scooters are other scooters. George often noticed when parking anywhere in or around campus, he could almost bet that within a few hours, there'd be another one parked alongside. By the end of the day, there'd be a few lined up.

George's scooter always stuck out from the bunch due to his feeble attempts to make it look more mod; it had a few extra rear-view mirrors, reflectors and pop-art decals stuck on it. He had no fear of anyone taking his scooter by mistake, other than perhaps the council's inorganic collection contractor.

But at least he and his fellow scooter riders parked their machines sensibly, George thought. Not like those moronic e-scooter riders who seem to wantonly litter the pavements, creating trip hazards with their childish e-toys that lacked any sense of style.

George could see some students were starting to set up the stage and sound gear at the café end of the courtyard. There was still a few hours before sound check so he took some time to experiment with his program. He sat down and began playing with SoundLive, flicking through screens, adjusting parameters and setting threshold levels. For the moment, he wanted relative quiet, but there was too much banging and crashing coming from the stage. He stood up and wandered slowly out of the university grounds and along the path into the reserve.

He was holding his laptop with one hand, fingers of the other occasionally tapping the keyboard, his eyes glued to the screen, headphones on, and his satchel dangling from his shoulder. He could vaguely see where he was going from his peripheral vision and felt his way across the ground with his feet. It never occurred to him just how nerdy he looked.

He had a small omnidirectional microphone clipped to the top of the screen of his laptop, which was taking in ambient sound from the environment for his acoustic environment analyser feature in SoundLive to model, and he monitored the readings on the screen as he walked.

He wandered off the path and made his way through a section of bush to get to the playing field beyond. In the middle of the bush was a secluded clearing about 20 metres in diameter. Focused on the laptop, he meandered across the flat open ground, completely oblivious to anything around him, when he clumsily tripped over a spaceship.

He sprawled on the ship's unseen metallic ramp, his laptop making a worrying clatter as it left his hand and scattered across the invisible surface. He got up on his knees and couldn't help notice that the laptop was hovering half a metre off the ground. He was off the ground himself, for that matter, a good 10 centimetres above it. He stood up and prodded the air with his foot. Definitely standing on something solid, he thought. He reached over and grabbed the laptop and then slowly retreated the way he'd come till he was on terra firma again.

George stood there looking at, or through, the invisible ramp like he was trying to solve a brainteaser. He bent down, scooped up a handful of dirt and threw it where he'd tripped. The dirt remained suspended across the ramp for a few seconds then disappeared. Being a bit of a sci-fi buff, George quickly deduced that this could be one of two things: either there was a space-time portal to a parallel universe, or someone had parked an invisible spaceship there.

He back-tracked to the edge of the clearing, opened his laptop and had another look at the acoustic environment analyser feature. He maximised the environment model image and fiddled with the reflection enhancement control until it went into saturation. Gradually a shape appeared on the screen. The image lacked detail, but George could see that the bulk of the shape was about two metres off the ground with four legs holding it up and a ramp at the point where he'd tripped. Yep, he thought, it's an invisible spaceship.

Meanwhile, on the other side of the world, word had got around about the strange rock and it had created a stir at San Fernando University, California.

"Sorry to bother you, John," Mike Hanley, head of geology, said as he entered his colleague's office, "but we've received some information regarding a seemingly rare type of mineral from New Zealand. Local data and test results conclude that it's an ancient meteor or asteroid fragment. They've conveniently nicknamed it Black Star. Funny thing is, it has powerful electromagnetic and isotope properties, but its physical make-up is not consistent with its atomic structure and nuclear behaviour. I just thought you might be interested."

John Davies was the director of nuclear sciences at the university and a member of the American Nuclear Society. "Where did you find this out?" he asked.

"University of Auckland, New Zealand. I'm told they found it buried in their grounds. They dug it up and they're studying it now. Anyway, they've got it up on their website and one of my students asked me about it."

"Noo Zealand? That's southern hemisphere, right?"

"I think so," Mike replied vaguely. "So a potentially unknown element possessing a dense structure and unstable atomic behaviour, it's got ANS written all over it, huh?"

"OK, I'll have a look. What's the website?"

"I've sent you the link in the email," Mike replied.

"Right. Here we go ... OK, nice picture ... Let's see, quartz-like, hardness 10 or greater, wow ... resonant properties ... hmm, this is interesting, they've got insulating properties similar to quartz, but electrical tests produce high resonant vibrations at different frequencies. Different frequencies? Man, some of these are off the scale. Do these guys know what they're doing? This is something like a huge piezo crystal, but with multiple resonant frequencies. That's weird."

"Yeah, and atomic make-up is also weird; seems they couldn't get a consistent reading."

"And of course being extraterrestrial, it's gotta be worth checking out. You know, there are theories about crystal electrical resonance and radioactivity behaviour basically working together to provide a highly efficient energy source. But no one's found the right material that optimises these behaviours," Davies explained.

"What sort of energy source?"

"Basically nuclear fission but at extremely low temperatures, but the direct output is more electromagnetic pulse energy rather than heat. The nuclear reaction is easily controllable and maintained indefinitely. That's the theory, anyway."

"Cool," Mike said, pretending he understood.

Davies continued, "Can work the other way, of course, and you end up with a super-nuclear device. And it would require very little material to do that."

"Oh yeah?"

"Mm. I mean, it's theory," Davies replied. "And the isotope separation would be highly involved, but still ..."

"If the theory's out there, we wouldn't want it to fall into the wrong hands, right?" Mike suggested.

"Exactly. Let me make some calls."

Chapter 6

George froze. He'd only taken a few steps inside the ship when suddenly, ahead of him, at the other end of the corridor, stood what was undoubtedly a creature from another planet. Or 'alien', or 'occupant from interplanetary craft' or whatever they were. There was no way this was some guy dressed up in an alien suit or a mannequin or oversized action figure. George was sure he would recognise an alien if he ever saw one, and he was looking at one right now. This was the real deal.

The corridor was tall and narrow, about ten metres from one end to the other. The floor was a light grey, with a sort of non-slip texture. The walls and ceiling consisted of segmented white panels that seemed to emanate artificial lighting from their surface. The exterior door, where George had come in, was positioned about halfway along the corridor. There wasn't any other detail that might suggest where the phasors were stored, or the spacesuits, or where the flight deck was or the hyperdrive. It was pretty much a featureless, grey-white, glowing corridor.

The figure also froze and was staring back at him. It was very tall, maybe two metres, slim and wearing a snug outfit that was a mix of dark greens, browns and blues in a kind of random camouflage pattern.

The creature's head and hands were exposed, and its mottled khaki skin was tough-looking with lots of fine lines. It was humanoid in shape with long slender arms and legs, two of each in the usual configuration. It wore black boots and a black belt with various small attachments fastened around its thin waist. Its head was somewhat triangular in shape with facial features similar to the human variety, but lacking in detail. Its eyes were quite large and dark. Its nose was rather flat with two horizontal slit-like nostrils. There were bumps on the side of its head where George would have expected ears, no hair or eyebrows, and its mouth was a lipless slit. George thought the alien looked kind of ugly, but in an elegant sort of way. He guessed it was probably quite strong and fast moving, and, in all likelihood, quite capable of ripping his arms off or sucking his brain out.

Of course, IQ thought George looked a little deficient. "What are you doing on my ship?" he said, barely moving his mouth.

George flinched as a series of bizarre images whirled around in his head. To George's ears, IQ's question sounded like a low-frequency grating sound with intermittent sharp crackles. Like some kind of rumbling radio interference from a broken set. But it was accompanied by some kind of sixth-sense message in his head.

George was doing a great impression of someone who had just met an alien from outer space for the first time. His mouth slowly gaped as his brain fumbled for a reality check. The rest of his body wanted to leap up the wall, but the sudden shock, or complete lack of preparation for this sort of eventuality, kept him stock-still. Real life doesn't really prepare us for this sort of scenario, he later thought. The only guidance for alien meet-and-greet protocol that George could think of was what they did in the movies. But in his panic-stricken state, he couldn't remember what that was.

"Ah ..." was all he could manage.

"What are you doing on my ship?" IQ repeated.

Between IQ and the navcom, they were sussing George out for suitable help. IQ would need someone familiar with the local surroundings and willing enough, or stupid enough, to help him get the Y2K. He needed someone he could trust and easily manipulate.

Again, as IQ spoke, another sequence of cryptic images raced through George's head to the tune of IQs grating speech.

George slowly raised his hand in greeting. "Hi, my name's George," he uttered with trepidation.

At this point, it was fifty-fifty as to whether George was to continue existing. IQ just had to think that George should be zapped into nothingness and the ship's in-built defence mechanism would happily oblige, without even making a mess. The navcom, however, rather liked him.

IQ took a step forward. "Look. Will you go away, please?" he said, motioning with his hand for George to go back the way he'd come.

George nearly turned inside out. It was one thing to come face to face with a creature from another planet and saying 'Hi'; it was another realising it could move towards you with menacing intent. George's own in-built defence mechanism kicked in and he cowered to the floor admirably.

"Oor ..." he whimpered, clutching his satchel.

"Ah shit!" IQ suddenly cried and whirled around and disappeared down the corridor.

George remained crouched for a bit, waiting to see what would happen next. Nothing did. It seemed the creature was alarmed at something. He slowly stood up and took a few steps forward. The corridor wasn't very long and ended at a T intersection. He hadn't noticed which way the creature went as he was too busy being a coward. He got to the junction. Both ways were a short distance and ended in a door. He went left. As it turned out, it was an excellent choice. It meant he'd stand a good chance of staying alive. He took a few more steps forward, then stopped and listened. Nothing. Not even a hum. He put his satchel down to get his phone out so he could video the event.

Just then, the door in front of him opened and he was flung outside. He sprawled on a dusty patch of bare ground and performed a rather ungainly tumble while flailing his arms about in an effort to fend off anything nasty as well as trying to control his crash-landing.

He poked his head up from his feeble defensive position and readied for some kind of evasive action, which probably would have involved running away quickly. However, nothing further appeared to be happening. He got up and gingerly stumbled back towards the ship with his arms outstretched. Eventually he reached the other side of the clearing. The ship wasn't there. Gone. He felt a pang of disappointment.

He looked around. The reality of the situation began to sink in. "Christ!" he eventually blurted out. And then, just to be sure, "Fuckin' hell!"

He heard voices. Just then, two kids came wandering out of the bush, one of them carrying a stick. They stared at George. He stared at them. He could tell they thought he looked a bit strange, particularly as he still had his arms outstretched.

After a puzzling pause, one of the kids asked, "What're you doing?'

"D-D-Did you see that?" cried George, waving his arms in the air.

That was it – the two kids were off. There was no way they were going to hang around with this nutter looking like a total moron and talking shit.

George stood there, vacantly gazing around, completely bewildered by it all. He swore a bit more, but it didn't seem to achieve much. Then he realised why the kids had looked concerned; he was covered in dust and dirt, from head to foot. He brushed himself down and it helped him to get into a more rational mood.

He couldn't believe what had just happened. It was almost fading like a dream. He felt it was the sort of thing he might have trouble telling anyone. 'A nasty alien ejected me from an invisible spaceship this morning, but I'm OK now' just didn't seem that plausible.

Pity I didn't get any video, he thought. "Oh shit, my bag!" he suddenly cried out.

He paced around the area beating around bushes in a futile fashion. Maybe those kids have it, he thought. He ran to the other side of the clearing, through the bush till he could see the playing field beyond. He could see the two kids walking across it, one of them waving a stick. But neither had his satchel.

George sighed. It's on the ship, he thought. I've left my bag on a spaceship and now it's gone. He kicked at a clump of dirt in frustration and then walked dejectedly back to the clearing where he stopped dead in his tracks, gobsmacked. Staring back at him, on the far edge of the clearing, was the homeless guy he and Steve had come across in the reserve and in the pub.

"Hello again," the old guy said. "Seen a ghost?"

George looked around him, trying to act casual. “Ah, no,” he said, slightly uncertain. He was pretty sure he hadn’t seen a ghost.

The old man came closer. “I think he’ll be back, you know.”

“Who’ll be back?” George replied, acting dumb.

The homeless guy held out his arm and motioned to where the ship had been. “Our friend,” he said with a big grin.

“Friend?” George queried, feeling a bit foolish that he was actually having this conversation.

The old man chuckled. “Oh yes, he’ll be back. Don’t worry.” He gazed up at where the spaceship had been. After a slight pause he suddenly broke into an insane grin. “Righto,” he said and turned to wander off.

It suddenly occurred to George that the old man somehow knew the spaceship was there. Had he been watching the whole time? George opened his mouth to respond; he had several questions trying to get out at once. In the end he said nothing. The old man was gone.

What stopped IQ from instructing his ship’s defence system to zap George into a billion bits was an alert from the proximity detector. Two individuals were approaching the ship.

“Ah shit,” IQ exclaimed. Time to go, he thought. He whirled round and headed back to the flight deck to look at taking evasive action. On the way, he instructed the navcom to deal with the undesirable, which it did in a decidedly humane way.

In fact, the navcom chose just the right moment to eject George so his satchel was left behind. The ship’s defence system had already disabled the phone and anything else in the satchel. The contents would certainly give IQ a few clues on what made this human tick.

He took the satchel onto the flight deck and emptied the contents on the console in front of his seat. He sat down and picked up the items one by one and examined them. He thought the laptop and phone were very retro-cool; clearly primitive technology with no style, but quaintly interesting. Ah, good ol' petroleum-based copolymers, he thought, feeling the surface of the laptop.

Next, he picked up the small bag of weed Steve had given George. Now this looks familiar, he thought. He got up, opened the medi-locker and took out the subatomic analyser, normally used for medical purposes, but can be used for pretty much anything. He opened the bag and inserted a small probe into it. Almost immediately the results were telecast into his head, also coming up on the flight console monitor screen.

He sat back in his seat and studied the 'Wiki-Worlds' report. Interesting fact, 101: 'Smoking can be damaging to the health of some species, including fleurian, aluminoid and human.' Damaging? IQ wondered. How can it possibly be damaging?

The report showed how to roll your own, so IQ, being a keen smoker, tried some cannabis from planet Earth. He sat back in his seat, lit up and puffed away. This is good shit, he thought.

Chapter 7

George made his way back to the university and greeted Steve halfway across the courtyard.

"How's it going?" Steve asked.

"Ah, OK," George said, gazing vacantly at the stage. He wanted to ask how Steve was going, getting the stage set up, but he was too dazed and confused to indulge in anything too coherent.

"Everything's all set," Steve said brightly. "You got your stuff?"

George thought for a moment. He felt naked without his satchel and completely lost without his laptop and phone. "Ah ..." was all he could manage at the moment.

Steve clocked George's distant expression. "What's up? Where's your gear?"

The recent events were replaying in George's brain. It all suddenly felt very surreal to him. He also felt embarrassed thinking about it. He still wasn't sure what he was going to say to Steve as he began to open his mouth to reply.

Luckily, Steve interrupted George's slow response. "Don't you need your computer?"

George snapped back to reality. His computer was in his satchel, which he left on the spaceship. Of course it was. But for God's sake, don't say that, he thought. "Yes, I do," he finally said.

"You gonna get it? We've got a couple of hours, there's still plenty of time," Steve said.

"Yeah ..." George said vaguely. He briefly thought about going back home and getting his desktop. Then he had an idea. "OK, maybe I'll try something. You got your phone?"

"Yep." Steve handed over his smart phone.

"Unlock it," George asked.

George prodded the touch-screen of Steve's phone and found the Wi-Fi connection to the stage. He then dialled up his website, logged in, selected remote access to his home computer and opened SoundLive.

A thought suddenly struck him. He exited from that and went into his global tracking app. His laptop and phone appeared to be nowhere. He felt another wave of disappointment and loss. He went back into SoundLive and fingered the touch-screen till he found Steve's playlist. Suddenly, a high-powered heavy metal number blasted forth from the PA. George fingered the screen a bit more, the sound level faded down a bit.

"Are you doing that?" Steve asked.

"Yeah."

"Cool. I got that song on my phone, I think."

"This is from your phone," George replied.

Steve was impressed. "Ah shit. Who needs front of house, eh?"

"OK." George shut the link and handed the phone back. "I can monitor the PA via the Wi-Fi link to the stage and dial in to my computer at home to access SoundLive. Unfortunately, they'll be no control, but that's OK, I'll just do some analytical stuff. You can use your hardware set-up for the main sound processing as usual."

Steve was satisfied with this. "Oh, cool. Didn't you want to use your laptop?"

George turned his head and gazed thoughtfully into the distance. "Long story," he eventually said. "So, we'll see how it goes, huh?" he added, hoping to give the impression that this had been the plan all along.

As the recent events whirled around in his brain, he could understand why folk who come across aliens from other planets go mad. Or at least why others think they've gone mad, so he certainly didn't want to start explaining the whole alien-stole-my-laptop thing.

"Shall we get a coffee or something?" Steve suggested.

"Yeah, great," George replied. A coffee sounded reassuring.

They wandered over to the student café and bought two coffees and sat at one of the outside tables.

"I thought SoundLive was nearly ready," Steve said.

"It is, but having a few hardware problems," George replied. Then he quickly changed the subject. "Hey, I wrote a new song."

"Yeah?"

"Yeah, I woke up this morning with this tune in my head. It's called 'Black Star'. And it's really cool."

"Ah-huh," Steve replied. "Fit in with what we do?"

"Of course. I mean, you could arrange it however you wanted, but we can certainly give it the Dark City treatment." George struck a thoughtful expression. "That's interesting, your name is Dark City, and the song is 'Black Star'. As in dark, black, black, dark."

"Yeah, I get it. There's a theme there. Well, at least I fit into that," Steve said, referring to his skin colour. "So what's the song about?"

"Well, currently, the theories of dream reality. Whatever that means. Or urban alienation," George said offhandedly.

Steve grinned. "Deep and meaningful stuff. "Sure to be a hit."

Just then Razor, Dark City's guitarist, came wandering over. "Hey," he greeted.

"Razor the laser. All right, dude?" asked Steve.

"Yeah, mate. How's it going, George?"

"Yeah, cool."

Razor's nick name was a jibe at his razor-sharp wit – he didn't really have any. He'd gained the name in high school and it stuck. His real name was Jeremy Ethan Osterburg-Pratt. He was average build with a mass of long, wavy, dark-brown hair and a short goatie. He looked a bit of a chilled-out hippy but could play a mean guitar.

"You doing your software thing?" he asked George.

"Yep. Working on my acoustic environment analyser feature. The idea is to analyse the surrounding reflection, diffusion and absorption qualities of the immediate environment and adjust the sound source for ideal balance."

"Oh yeah?" Razor said with a slight chuckle. "Sounds like fun."

"Oh, it's fun all right."

"Hey, look at this," Razor said, looking to change the subject. He held out his arm, pulled up his shirtsleeve, revealing a tattoo.

"New one, is it?" Steve asked.

"Yep."

"Very symbolic."

George was less than impressed. "Well done," he said flatly. "I'm sure it will make all the difference." Just then, something caught his eye. "Won't be a minute." He stood up and left the table. "Charley!"

She was about to go into the café when George called.

“Hi, George,” she said with a wave. “You here to see the gig?”

“Kind of. I’m doing a few sound experiments for my third-year project.”

“Great. What did you think of the Black Star?”

George’s brain flipped – not for the first time that day. “Black Star?”

“Yeah. The rock we excavated near the main entrance,” Charley explained.

George knew what she was talking about, but for the moment he held his vacant expression.

Charley continued. “You were there the other day looking at it with that Scottish guy.”

“Yes.” Finally George registered. “Ah! That was you in the pit?”

“Yes.”

“Sorry, I didn’t recognise you with all that gear on,” he said. “So what is it about Black Star?”

“That’s the name we gave it. It’s black and it comes from space.”

“Right,” George replied thoughtfully. He glanced back over at Steve and Razor. “Hey, listen, I better get back. Do you want to catch up after the gig? You can tell me all about the Black Star.”

“Sure. How about we meet up here?” she suggested.

“See you then,” he said and wandered back to rejoin the group.

“Oi, oi,” Razor said as George approached. “Who’s that chick?”

“That’s Charley.”

George had met Charley in a computer graphics class last year. She was a bit shorter than him with blonde, shoulder-length hair, very pretty and one year younger. They’d gone out a couple of times, or at least hung out casually, usually with other friends, but they were both too shy to really get to know one another.

He assumed she preferred hanging out with her geeky girlfriends, so he kept his distance. But the reality was Charley liked George – there was a certain eccentricity about him that made up for his geekiness. She knew she was a bit of a geek herself and therefore maybe they were compatible.

"So who is she?" Steve asked mischievously.

George grappled his way back to the conversation. "Oh, you know, this girl I know," he said in an offhand way. "We met last year."

Razor shook his head in mock disapproval. "You're such a flirt, George." He stood up. "I'm going to get a coffee."

George quickly changed the subject. "Are you doing a sound check?" he asked Steve.

"Yep, Seconds to Go are setting up now," Steve replied, looking over his shoulder at the stage. The courtyard was beginning to fill with students.

"OK ..." said George. He still came across looking a bit distant.

"Are you all right?" Steve asked.

"Well ..." George began.

He was desperately trying to think of the most convincing way of telling someone that he'd just met an alien from outer space. His brain was giving him a number of options, and he wasn't that fussed with any of them. "Fine," he eventually said.

George knew he would have to tell Steve about his alien encounter at some point. Maybe he'd save the story for the next time they were pissed. That way, there'd be an easy out if he was questioned about it later – he'd just say he was pissed. But for now, he decided to keep the conversation to everyday reality. "You guys all set for the Summer Sizzler gig?" he asked Steve.

"Yeah, mate. It's gonna be brilliant. You keen to play?"

"Sure. If you want me to."

"Absolutely."

George didn't always play in Dark City gigs, but Steve figured George's synth would help project the sound out to a large festival crowd.

"So you've had a bit of practice then?" George asked.

"A bit. But if things start coming apart, Matt usually holds it together."

"Oh yeah. Matt the mad drummer," said George with a grin.

"Any dodgy moments and Matt goes ape-shit. Takes the attention away from any screw-ups."

George forced a laugh. "A man of many talents. So, let me know when you want to rehearse."

"We should do something next week, eh," Steve replied. "And we can nail down our set. There's a Sizzler planning meeting tonight, by the way."

Just then Razor came back. He put his coffee down and pulled out his cigarettes and thumped them on the table. He took a seat and lit up. He knew that neither George nor Steve smoked cigarettes, and he had no worries about smoking when in the company of non-smokers. He even had no worries in smoking in smoke-free zones, and this was one of them.

"Er, this is a smoke-free area," George informed him.

"That's cool, George. I'm OK if you don't smoke." He blew a lungful into the air.

"Well, call me presumptuous, but I think that includes you, too," George explained, pointing to the sign.

Razor took another drag and blew it out again. "Yeah, I suppose so," he said, admitting defeat. He reached over and stubbed the cigarette out on a nearby raised garden wall.

Steve pointed to the ghastly health effects illustration on the cigarette packet. "Look. That's not going to do your guitar playing any good."

"Well, I ain't got that, have I?" Razor replied.

"Not yet," George said.

"That's right," Razor said. "Anyway, you buggers can talk, smoking that wacky-backy."

"That's medicinal," Steve said.

"So's this," Razor replied, holding his cigarette up.

"Wouldn't call that medicinal," George said, pointing at the cigarette packet.

"No, but like I said, I ain't got that, have I?" Razor argued.

There was a slight pause before Steve concluded, "And another Dark City deep and meaningful discussion comes to its logical conclusion." He stood up. "I better get back over there."

"Can I borrow your phone?" George asked him.

"Sure," Steve said and handed it over.

George and Razor also got up to leave.

"I wrote a new song," George said.

"Oh, yeah?"

"I call it 'Black Star'."

"Isn't there already a song called that?" Razor asked.

"Is there? One more won't hurt."

"Not if it's crap," Razor said with a laugh. He lit up the remains of his cigarette. "By the way, you've got shit in your hair," he said as he headed for the stage.

George quickly brushed his hands through his hair and, sure enough, bits of twigs and leaves flew in all directions. He was embarrassed to think what Charley must have thought. He pocketed Steve's phone and went off in the direction of the reserve. He felt the need to retrace the steps he'd made earlier in order to try and make sense of things. If the whole surreal notion of the spaceship, or whatever it was, wasn't enough, that old tramp with the mad grin seemed to acknowledge its presence as if it was an everyday occurrence for him.

George felt he needed answers. He needed to determine whether or not he was going loopy or if an extraterrestrial event did occur here not forty-five minutes ago. Plus he was hoping to find the old man.

He got to the landing site and wandered around looking for clues. At times he stretched his arms out, trying to feel for a spaceship, but there was nothing. He did, however, recognise his scuff marks from where he hit the ground. And there seemed to be four depressions in the dirt, presumably from spaceship landing gear. Although the longer he studied them, the more they simply looked like any other piece of dirt in the area.

He got Steve's phone out and dialled up his device tracker again. Still nothing. Suddenly he had a creepy feeling that he was being watched. He quickly scanned the clearing perimeter. Nothing. He then stood still for a few seconds, listening. He could hear Seconds To Go doing their sound check from the courtyard.

Feeling rather dejected, he started to wander back to the courtyard so he could rejoin the human race. He was at the bottom of path that led up to the university boundary, when he noticed movement down the intersecting path to the motorway bridge. It was the same homeless guy. He watched him for a few seconds until he disappeared round the bend.

Seconds To Go were into their set when George returned. He dialled into his website and did a few adjustments in SoundLive that controlled the PA through the Wi-Fi; nothing drastic, just a few EQ tweaks. The latency was ridiculous and he really needed to do this trial with his laptop. Still, it looked promising, he thought.

During the break between Lazy Brain and Foulmouth, there was another ground tremor. Not serious, but somehow it affected the sound system. George couldn't work out if the problem was in the PA, Wi-Fi link or SoundLive itself. The main problem was noise – there seemed to be some kind of static coming in and out of the sound.

While George fiddled with his SoundLive, Charley sidled up to him and they had a brief shouting match at each other before George yelled, "I'll see you later."

"Yes," Charley yelled back. "At the café."

George gave the thumbs up and went over to the side of the stage to see Steve before he went on. He closed the remote access link and handed the phone back to him. He could still hear the strange static noise, but people didn't seem to notice or care, and Steve's band managed to obliterate any sense of reasonable sound balance anyway.

Once the polite applause had died down, George went over to the café to catch up with Charley and found her with a group of her friends.

"That went pretty well," she said, full of enthusiasm.

George had been focusing on SoundLive the whole time and hadn't really been taking any notice of the music. "Yeah," was the best he could come up with.

"I like Seconds To Go best. What did you think?"

He was desperately trying to remember which band they were. "They're OK."

Charley beamed at him, waiting for him to deliver some kind of intelligent observation on the proceedings. It obviously wasn't forthcoming. He seemed distracted.

"What are you up to now?" she asked.

George just wanted to go home, switch on his desktop computer, open SoundLive and give it a big hug. Instead he shrugged and said, "Nothing much."

"Wanna go get a drink?" Charley asked. "O'Dougal's. Irish Bar, round the corner."

She figured that most of the students would go to The Space Cadet opposite campus and the Irish bar should be a bit quieter. How wrong she was.

The place was swinging with a small Irish band at the far end of the bar going full flight. The band played fiddle, bodhrán, bouzouki and bass guitar, and they all boisterously belted out unintelligible nonsense like their life depended on it. The small crowd was joining in the sing-song with severe gusto, most improvising their own inebriated lyrics. It was a tumultuous racket.

George and Charley paused just inside the door, looking slightly shell-shocked. George almost expected the place to suddenly go quiet and for everybody to turn and stare at them, but no such luck.

Charley looked up at him in surprise then burst out laughing. "Come on," she yelled. "Let's grab a Guinness."

They'd just got their drinks and were searching for a suitably discreet place to sit when there was a very loud, "Aye, Georgie boy," to George's right.

George flinched, then turned to face a very drunk Scotty.

"Ya comb tae see hoe thee other harlf live, eh boyo?" he yelled, each syllable spraying beer in several directions.

"Hi, Scotty. Guinness today." George held up his glass. "Cheers."

"Aye, cheers mon. Hoe are ye, darlin'?" Scotty yelled at Charley. "'Ere, ya batter wotch oat fer thus fella," he gestured at George. "Sly wee one. Aye," he said with a wink.

"Wouldn't have thought this place would be your scene. Got a bit of Irish in you, eh, Scotty?" George asked, pretending to be having a good time.

"Aye, ah bin comin' here fer years. Ah fookin' awn th plearce, met. Ha ha, aye boyo."

Just then, the band started up the next song and Scotty turned to face them, held his beer in the air and began bellowing out random, incomprehensible drivel along with the rest of the pissheads.

"We'll be over there," George gestured to the other end of the pub. But Scotty didn't hear; he was too busy roaring away like fury.

They were halfway through their Guinnesses when the band finally took a break and the crowd's singing tapered off. The pair had found an empty booth where they could hold a meaningful conversation.

"So, that rock on campus," George asked. "You're studying that, are you?"

"Yes. In geology," Charley replied. "It's really weird. Unusual properties. And you know those tremors?"

"Yeah."

"Well that thing makes them. It has some kind of resonance that has a life of its own. It's almost like it's alive."

George thought about retelling his theory about lava cave resonances but wisely decided not to. "You call it Black Star?"

"Yes. It's just a name."

"Right," George looked away thoughtfully. "By coincidence, I woke from a dream this morning with a tune in my head and the title was 'Black Star'. So I got up and wrote it down." He paused. "I play keyboards," he explained, mimicking playing a piano.

“Yes, I know.” She looked puzzled. “Isn’t there already a song called ‘Black Star’?”

“Probably. But not like this one.”

“I’ll have to hear it sometime,” she said out of politeness. “It’s a strange rock, though. Really weird. And so hard. Unbelievably hard. I actually managed to chip a piece off and looked at it under a magnifying glass and it, like, swirls.”

“Swirls?”

“Yeah. The inside of the stuff swirls. Like, I dunno, smoke or mist.”

George gazed into his beer. “A bit like this Guinness.”

Charley smiled and raised her glass. “Well anyway, cheers!”

“Cheers!” George responded. If all else fails, he thought, just get pissed.

Although he wasn’t ready to tell his close-encounter story just yet, he did feel a sense of support from Charley. And she, likewise, was quite happy to tell him about her swirly chip.

Suddenly a rollicking version of ‘Whiskey in the Jar’ erupted from the far end of the bar and the place went mad.

Chapter 8

George parked his scooter under the lean-to at the back of his flat, switched it off and sat there for a bit. He lived in an old two-bedroom wooden villa with a steep-pitched corrugated-iron roof, built in the early part of the twentieth century on a quarter-acre subdivided section. It was just like many others in the neighbourhood, about 10 minutes from the central city.

He was renting the house along with his flatmate, Greg, who was rarely around due to his travelling sales job, and he was presently away down country for a few days. The house was owned by Greg's mother and she gave the two boys a cheap rental deal. It was a bit run down but certainly had a lot more character than the high-rise student apartments in the city.

George sat on his scooter with a bunch of mixed feelings floating around in his head. He felt rather dejected about losing his laptop and phone. They were insured. But how was he going to explain their loss to anyone? He'd have to think of a lie. Insurance companies would be used to that, surely. He certainly couldn't face retelling his meeting-an-alien story. He felt foolish just thinking about it. It felt so out of context with everyday life, it was almost like it never happened. In fact, during his time with Charley earlier, he did indeed forget about it for a while.

He had enjoyed his time with Charley that evening and decided he should try and see her more often.

He sighed, dismounted, pulled his helmet off and placed it on the seat. He had a few minutes to gather together a copy of SoundLive before heading off to the Summer Sizzler meeting. He slowly scuffed his way down the path, past the long grass that used to be a lawn, but now concealed a number of cannabis seedlings, and up the steps to the back door. As he approached it, he flicked through his keys. He looked up, poised with the door key, and nearly did a backflip. There, by the back door, was his canvas satchel.

George stared at it, his mind racing. Surely, he thought, only one person, or thing, could have put that there. Did he, or it, come here? To my flat? All sorts of creepy feelings started firing his imagination. Maybe it's still here, he thought. Maybe it's inside waiting for me.

He suddenly felt conspicuous. He looked around. Twilight was settling in and things were starting to look a bit scary. He stared at the satchel for a while longer, half expecting to finally realise that all the unusual activity of the day was suddenly going to be explained in a clear, logical and believable way, and he would be able to say with immense relief something like, "Oh, that's all right then." And go in and watch the telly.

He wished he could turn back time. He was sure he'd handle the whole thing differently. Maybe next time, he thought. Let's put this down to lessons learned when meeting aliens from outer space for the first time.

Facing up to reality, George leaned towards the door and put the key in the lock as quietly as he could. A deck board squeaked loudly under his foot as he put weight on it. He felt as though the whole world heard it. It was like a signal to the monster aliens; when they hear the squeaky floorboard, that's when they come and get you.

Once his heart restarted, he gingerly unlocked the door and opened it, very slowly, with just enough gap to peek his head round and survey what was inside. He was all too aware of the racket he was making. Why is it, he thought, just when you think you've got a brain-eating alien waiting inside your house, the door hinges shriek like a banshee, the floorboards squeak underfoot and the can full of nails that you left above the door comes crashing down?

In his terror-stricken state, George had forgotten about the can of nails. It was his ingenious and rather cheap burglar alarm. It hung precariously above the door on the inside, but could be armed and disarmed with a pull on a string from the outside. It had only just missed his head as it came crashing to the floor. The noise was enough to waken the dead.

George froze in sheer panic. He listened for anything nasty, his senses on edge. To his horror, he heard, no felt, something pounding towards him. It took him a few seconds to realise it was his own heartbeat.

All was quiet, in fact. There were no reassuring background noises, like lawnmowers, or kids playing down the street, or traffic going by, to conveniently put things into perspective. It was at times like this he wished he had a dog. A big, friendly, loyal dog that would rescue him in times of trouble. Like when space aliens visit.

He scanned inside. His eyes were becoming accustomed to the dim interior. As far as he could see, his kitchen and living room looked normal. He reached in and turned on the light. He paused. Still nothing to suggest his house was occupied. Not a sound. Other than his wild imagination, which just wouldn't shut up.

The vague notion of having to make a move at some point started to interrupt this process of skilful investigation; he was going to have to go in. He bent down, picked up his satchel and stepped inside. His foot scrunched on nails, but he'd passed the point of no return. He half tiptoed across the floor, had a quick look around and put his satchel on the kitchen table.

So far so good. He moved quietly around the rest of the house, turning lights on as he went. It was all clear. He went back into the kitchen, closed the door, sat down at the table and opened his satchel. Everything seemed to be in there. One by one, he removed the contents and laid them out. Laptop, microphone, phone, charger, USB stick, pen, notepad, TV remote, small plastic bag that was noticeably empty of hash, muesli bar...

TV remote? He didn't remember putting that in there. Why would he put the TV remote in his bag? He looked inside again. Nope, that's it; empty. But no hash. What happened there? he wondered.

He shoved everything back in except the remote, which he went to return to its rightful place on the coffee table. However, halfway across, he couldn't help notice that it was still there, right where he'd left it the night before.

He stared at the remote on the coffee table. He stared at the one in his hand. They were identical. He pointed the one he'd got from his bag at the TV and pressed the ON button. It wouldn't press down. He tried a few more buttons. They all seemed to be fake. He turned it over and tried opening the battery cover. It wouldn't open; it was outlined, but moulded as part of the body. It was a replica remote. The same weight and size, same physical appearance, but totally non-functional. He picked up the one on the coffee table and turned the

TV on. It worked.

Thank God, he thought, something normal for a change. He turned it off.

He went back to the table, sat down and studied the fake remote for a while and desperately racked his brain as to where it had come from. He thought about using a TV remote to control live sound. He was planning a phone app for SoundLive but hadn't considered using a TV remote. The notion of each person in a live audience with their own remote being able to control the stage sound for their own comfort. Silly idea really, he thought.

"Shit!" George suddenly blurted out as he remembered the Summer Sizzler meeting. He glanced at the time. A quarter past eight. The meeting was at 8.30; better get going, he thought. He whipped his laptop out of his bag, opened it and turned it on.

"Come on, come on," he muttered as it was booting up. At last he was able to enter his password and check SoundLive. Yep, still there. Good. He closed the laptop, shoved it in his bag, grabbed his keys, rushed to the door, swung it open and ran smack into IQ.

George stared up at him from the floor. "Jesus Christ!" he yelled. This was it. This is what it was all leading to. He was absolutely right to expect the worst because it was actually happening. He was about to get eaten, zapped, or turned inside out, or his brains sucked out, or some such horrible way of death by alien.

"Get up and let's go. Where's the telesender?" IQ's grating squawks announced themselves along with the usual series of mind-blowing hieroglyphics in George's brain.

George stared up at IQ. "What do you want?" he whimpered.

"The telesender," IQ repeated. He pointed to it on the

table. "That thing."

George scrambled to his feet and picked up the remote. "The TV remote? Is it yours?"

"Bring it, and let's go," squawked IQ.

George had no idea what IQ was saying. "You want this? What is it?" he said, jiggling it like a drumstick.

IQ lurched forward. "Careful with that," he said. "Give it here and let's go."

To George's surprise, IQ snatched the remote from his hand, turned and strode easily out the back door and down the steps.

George dawdled as he desperately tried to juggle conflicting signals. He was trying to figure out what IQ had said, but part of his brain simply refused to believe in anything that was going on right now. However, he had caught the 'Let's go' part of what IQ had said.

"Let's go where?" he asked as he gingerly followed IQ out to the back porch.

"Come on!" IQ said impatiently.

George got the message to move it. He quickly ran back inside to the table, grabbed his satchel and shot out of the house.

As IQ made his way down the path, he paused and pointed at the long grass. "You had some of that in your bag. Can I have some more?"

George detected that there was a question but wasn't exactly sure what it was. He quickly conjured up a suitably vague answer. "Oh yeah ..."

IQ looked at him, expecting more. He then continued in his loping gait towards the spaceship.

"Bloody hell!" exclaimed George and nearly did another backflip as he looked up at IQ's ship hovering above the next-door neighbour's garden.

This time he could see it plain as day. IQ was allowing

him visual access. It was about twice the size of a double-decker bus. But, unlike a double-decker bus, it was obviously designed and built with interstellar travel in mind. It had a cool retro appearance about it, but was also very sleek; a bit like a giant, space-age purple '57 Chevy. It had a rounded front-end and a finned back-end and neat lines of chrome trim. It didn't have much other detail; the windows, for example, were the same colour as the body. It was suspended in the air and totally silent.

As George stared up at it, a thought occurred to him. "Now hang on. Are you abducting me?"

IQ detected the concern in George's voice. "We're not going far. I need your help," he said in his squawking tones.

George caught a vague call-for-assistance vibe from IQ's request and he tentatively followed. The spaceship descended silently until it was a couple of metres off the ground. A thin, metallic ramp silently unfolded itself from the underside of the craft, neatly avoiding the wooden paling fence between George's place and the neighbours. George followed IQ up the ramp. If he had any doubts about his initial close encounter with IQ, this settled it – it was now a definite fourth-kind scenario, he thought. Or maybe three-and-a-half kind, as he wasn't sure if this was an abduction or an invitation. What the hell. In for a penny ...

Chapter 9

IQ led George down the main corridor and onto the flight deck. Upon entering, the first thing that caught George's attention was the main console and monitor screen. The console swept round in a gentle curve at the front of the flight deck from one side to the other. It was mainly black and had two tiers lined with chrome trim along its rounded edges. The bottom tier seemed to be dedicated to controls, mostly black, but also a few coloured buttons and knobs, all laid out in neat segmented groups.

The narrower top tier was alive with a kaleidoscope of multicoloured indications. Beyond that, the large monitor screen swept right around, just like a massive wrap-around windscreen. It was used as a window as well as a monitor. It currently displayed a bird's-eye view of George's flat. At each end of the screen were small quarter-light windows.

The ceiling had a similar style to the console in that it had two layers that followed the curvature of the room with rounded edges and chrome trim. Subtle lighting emanated between the ceiling tiers, creating an eerie, dim glow about the place, and it took a few minutes for George's eyes to adjust. The side panelling and doors were mainly purple with various black fittings and chrome highlights. The floor appeared to be a similar material to the corridor floor except it was black with shiny speckles through it.

There were two sliding doors a few metres apart on the rear wall of the flight deck; IQ and George entered through one of these. A couple of metres in from the door was the centrally positioned pilot seat, looking much like a black dentist chair with various implements suspended on one side and from the ceiling above it. There was not much floor space; it was obviously designed and built to accommodate one pilot but there were couch-like protrusions moulded into each side wall. IQ indicated to George to sit on one of these.

IQ sat sideways on the pilot's seat, facing George. Initially he said nothing ... that George could detect, anyway. George suddenly realised he was in the alien's domain. He felt like a foreigner trapped in a foreign land, and he had to concentrate hard to stay rational about the whole thing.

He looked around the interior, desperate to think about cool scientific stuff. The interior was indeed quite striking with its moody lighting and chic design and the obviously advanced technology. In fact, he was quite mesmerised as he was suspended in a surreal moment until a change in scene suddenly appeared on the monitor screen and snapped his brain to attention. It was an aerial view of the university. IQ turned in his seat and sat back, facing the screen. The picture zoomed in on the rock in the campus courtyard.

"I need that," he squawked.

"Oh, the rock," George replied, not fully understanding IQ's wish.

IQ was still silently looking at him.

This is awkward, thought George. "Do you know what it is?" he asked.

"I need that," IQ repeated. "And I want you to help me. The navcom insists you are suitable."

They both looked at each other briefly, each trying to determine what the other was thinking. George couldn't believe he was again face to face with an alien from outer space and started feeling a panic attack coming on.

He shook his head in an effort to clear it. It seemed to do the trick. "OK ..." he said, not realising what he was agreeing to. He was then surprised that IQ mimicked his own head shaking.

IQ faced the screen. The picture zoomed back out till it displayed the entire courtyard.

"Can I ask a question?" George said, holding his hand up slightly.

IQ ignored him; he was busy conferring with the navcom.

George continued. "What is it with the TV remote?" he asked, pointing to the fake remote that IQ had put on the flight deck console.

IQ gave no reaction.

George waited for a few seconds. "This thing," he asked again, waving at the remote. "What is it?"

"Leave it," IQ said, and re-engaged with the navcom.

George couldn't read the answer in his head, so he tried again. "But what is it?" he said, pointing at it again.

IQ snatched up the remote and held it up to George's face. George's face grimaced as if it was preparing for a left hook.

"This is a multi-state telesender. It's used to send stuff. I used it to locate your home and send your bag there. It can copy any state or form and it chose your TV remote," IQ explained. He sat back in his seat. "And it remained in your bag so I could find you."

George caught the gist of it in that there was indeed

an explanation, but he had no idea what it was. He noticed the view had changed through the windows. He leant over to the nearest one and saw they were hovering above the university. In his preoccupation with awe, imminent panic attacks and communication difficulties, he had failed to notice the craft rise, accelerate, decelerate and generally hover about the place. The new location suddenly reminded him of the Summer Sizzler meeting. "Hey, I don't suppose you can drop me off, can you? Down there," he said, pointing at the screen.

IQ ignored George's request. "I'll need you to put it on the Y2K."

They both looked at each other in a brief silent pause.

George had no idea what the alien was on about and ventured forth with his rudimentary alien communication skills. "You know, at times I can kind of sense what you're saying. Like some kind of telepathic thing. You know what I mean? You're telling me to do something, right? You want something ..."

The screen zoomed in on the rock.

"Oh! The rock! You want the rock!"

This time IQ didn't seem to argue, so maybe they were getting somewhere. "You know it's called Black Star," he informed helpfully.

Chapter 10

Once IQ was confident his plan was going to work, he began to explain it to George. "Here's what we'll do," he said. "I'll take us down so you can get out and go put the telesender on the Y2K. OK?"

George wasn't sure if that was it and paused before he answered. "Sorry, what was that?"

"Oh boy," sighed IQ. "This is going to be tough. I shall repeat."

"Huh?"

"Hang on ..." sighed IQ, getting slightly exasperated.

"You want to get the rock," said George.

"The rock, yes! You put the telesender on or near the Y2K," IQ explained, wrongly thinking they were finally making progress.

George replied with a blank stare.

"Got that?" IQ asked. "Right, let's do it." He prepared to get out of his seat.

"I take it you can breathe our air," George said randomly. "Come to think of it, I can breathe the air in your spaceship," he said as he looked around, in an effort to emphasise the point.

They gazed at each other momentarily.

IQ shrugged. "Big deal," he said, not particularly caring about whatever George was saying.

"So does that mean your planet is similar to ours?" George persisted. "I mean, in terms of atmosphere."

"Right, let's go!" IQ called out, hoping to get George fired up. He leapt out of his seat, leaving George rather lost.

"Can I go now?" George asked and pointed to the screen. "Can you drop me off there?"

"Correct," said IQ. "We get the Y2K. Let's go."

George knew IQ was still talking about the rock but did not understand his role in the plan. "It's just that it's going to take a while to get that thing. I imagine it's very heavy, and I need to go to a meeting, you see. Can we do this later?"

IQ was trying hard to be patient. "Listen. Try to understand, all you have to do is put the remote on the rock. Right? How hard can that be? I can't. If I go out there, I'll be seen. OK? Humans will freak. It's vitally important that we do this very discreetly. Got it?"

George would be the first to agree that trying to converse with an alien from outer space was bound to have its difficulties, and he was getting quite bewildered by it all.

Suddenly, IQ got up and went over to the galley. He figured he needed something else to help break the ice.

Now what? George thought.

IQ rummaged around a bit, getting something out of a panel in the wall, then returned to his seat. He held up George's meagre stash.

"Hey, that's mine," George said.

"I like this," IQ said. And to George's astonishment, he rolled a joint and lit up. He took a deep drag. The smoke took a long time to be exhaled.

What the hell, George thought; when in Rome. He reached out for the joint. IQ didn't offer. He wasn't familiar with the concept of sharing.

"May I?" George asked as he very delicately took it from IQ's fingers. He took a drag himself and passed it back.

George didn't consider himself a smoker as such, but he did enjoy the odd puff on a joint. There was something medicinal about it. It enabled him to 'bounce back', so to speak. It helped him realise things aren't as bad as they seem.

Rev 3s, on the other hand, have cast-iron lungs. Smoking is big in the Sirius system – always has been – and rev lungs have got so used to smoking over the millennia that they've evolved into being completely immune to its ill effects. So much so that they could pretty much breathe anything and get away with it. A potentially deadly mixture of nicotine, tar, carbon dioxide and various other poisonous gases that come with smoking cigarettes, they could cope with just fine. A 78% nitrogen, 21% oxygen, 1% miscellaneous mix of air from planet Earth was perfectly fine, too.

"I like this," IQ said, looking at the joint between is fingers. "This is good shit."

George reached over again and this time IQ offered the joint.

"Does the job, eh," said George. "I can get some more if you want."

"You have some in your backyard," IQ pointed out.

"They're just seedlings. But yeah, no problem. I can get some more for you," said George. Then he added with a cheeky grin, "Duty free, no less."

The flight deck was getting quite cloudy, when George suddenly realised, "Hey! We can understand each other!"

"Yes, you're right. I can understand you as well. Interesting," IQ said, holding the joint up and eyeing it.

"Before, I would get images in my head about what you said," George explained, "but there was, like, big gaps in the message, you know?"

"Yes, same," said IQ. "The effect of this stuff is very interesting. Makes everything hazier but clearer." He handed it back to George.

"Have you smoked before?" George asked.

"Yes. Very common where I come from."

"Where is that exactly?"

"Sirius C Major."

George had no idea where that was, other than outer space. "Right. Well, look, my name's George," he said and held out his hand.

IQ looked at it. "Why?"

George shrugged. "I know it's a bit of an old-fashioned name, but that's what my parents named me. You kind of don't get any choice, you know? My mum was a great Beatles fan and her favourite was George Harrison. But it suits me. Don't you think? Shake, dude," he said as he waved his hand at IQ.

IQ held out his hand and waved it about.

Close enough, thought George. "Do you have a name?" he asked.

"I am IQ," said IQ as he waved his hand about again.

George couldn't help notice that IQ had two thumbs, with two very long fingers in between. Conveniently, his other hand was the same.

"Eye-queue? Cool name," George said.

"No, no, it's IQ," IQ explained.

"Oh, right. So now we're out of it and can understand each other, do you mind explaining what we're doing here?"

"I've come here to get the Y2K – that rock down there," IQ explained. "And I want you to help me."

"Why would you want to do that?" George asked.

"I need it for fuel. It can power my ship. In fact, a chunk that size will power it forever."

"How does it do that?"

"Partial particle accela-tronics. A bit like controlled nuclear fusion, but harnessing billions of tiny reactions instead of one huge reaction," IQ explained. "And at room temperature."

"Cool," said George, pretending to understand.

Thankfully, the navcom was keeping remarkably quiet. IQ could do without any smart alec comments about how things worked just now.

"What sort of rock is it?" George asked.

"Y2K. So I want you to put the TV remote on the rock so I can telesend it into the transfer bay."

"You can do that?"

"Yes."

George was impressed. "That's awesome." Then a thought occurred to him – Y2K sounded familiar. Where had he heard that before?

"So why do you need me?" he asked. "Why not just do the telesend thing yourself?"

"I'll be seen," IQ replied. "You'll be less conspicuous. Besides," he added, "I think someone else is after it."

"Someone else?"

"Yes, so we need to act quickly," IQ said.

"Do you know who?"

"Who what?"

"Who's after it?"

"I don't know at this point. They are still far away. They haven't reached the habitable zone yet," IQ explained.

George thought for a second. "What habitable zone?"

IQ was beginning to wonder if George was up to carrying out a simple task at all. "The one where your planet is," he said slowly. "Don't worry, once they realise I have it, I'll be in the next system."

"You mean someone from outer space?"

"That's right."

"Really?" George was becoming a little worried. "Another alien? Is it dangerous?"

"I don't know," IQ replied. "But it won't matter anyway."

George was uneasy about the situation. "You mean it won't matter to you. Yeah, ah, look, I dunno. Don't you have a tractor beam or something?"

"A what?"

"You know, a gravitational beam thing that draws things in. Like on *Star Wars*," George explained.

"Are you kidding? Do you know how expensive those things are? Besides, it'll never fit into a ship this size," IQ replied. He then sucked in the last of the joint, quite literally – the last of the dog-end disappeared down his throat.

George realised that once the cannabis effects wore off they'd struggle to understand each other again. Suddenly an alarm went off.

"The proximity," said IQ. "We need to ascend." He instructed the navcom accordingly.

On the screen George could see vehicles and machinery being brought into the courtyard. "Looks like they're bringing in a crane," he said.

They watched on the screen and after a while it was apparent that the workmen were just parking the machinery in the courtyard overnight in preparation for work the next day. The problem was the crane took up IQ's parking space.

"I need to land to drop you off," he said.

"Well, there's the car park, which is still full of cars, or the playing field, but there's a game on," said George helpfully. "Can you go back to the reserve – where you landed before?"

Just then, a bird's eye view of the reserve clearing came up on the monitor.

"Seems OK," said IQ. "I'll take it down."

George took his phone out of his bag and studied it for a few seconds. "No signal," he said. "I was going to call my mate to get some more weed."

"You'll have to go outside," said IQ.

"Yeah, once we've landed."

"We've landed. The ramp's down."

"Oh!" said George, rather surprised at the totally silent and still landing. He gathered his bits and headed out of flight deck and down the corridor. The external door was already open, and George strode down the ramp while monitoring his phone's signal strength. Sure enough the signal came right and he hit the call button. "Yo, Steve," he said into it.

"George. What's happening, man?"

"Ah, listen, you got any spare weed?"

"Yeah, sure. Wanna come over later on?"

"Can you come over here? Like, now?"

"I'm at the Summer Sizzler meeting. Should be outta here in an hour, I guess," said Steve. "I thought you were going to be here?"

"Just tied up with something. Can you ask if they want me to do anything? I dunno ... main desk, stage monitors ..."

"Sure. I'll let you know how it goes," Steve replied.

"Great, I'll see you later."

"My place at, say, ten?" Steve suggested.

"I'll call. OK? Bye." George hung up and was about to walk back up the ramp when he noticed movement on the far side of the clearing. He squinted in the dim of the twilight and could make out a shape. A grinning shape. It came forward and grinned at him.

"Hello, there," the grin said. It was the old homeless guy again.

"Hi," said George as he stopped at the foot of the ramp. He guessed the old man couldn't see IQ's ship so he didn't want to give the game away by walking up an invisible ramp.

"Ain't she a beauty?" the old man enthused.

"What is?" George asked, acting dumb.

"This!" said the old man, gesturing at the ship. "I can see it, you know."

"Ah ... OK," said George, unsure of what to do next.

"Can I talk to your friend?" the old man asked, nodding his head in the direction of the ship's open door. "There's something he should know."

George dithered. "Wait here." He ran up the ramp.

IQ was waiting in the corridor.

"He can see the ship," said George.

"I know. We'll have to leave."

"Can you give me the telesender and I'll go and put it on the rock?"

IQ paused for a moment. "Yes." He went back onto the flight deck and grabbed the telesender off the console.

It was then the navcom finally piped up. *Well, actually, the Y2K is still half buried. The telesend may not work. In fact, if it resonates during the telesend, it could be dangerous.*

That stopped IQ in his tracks. He stood there on the flight deck thinking, when George came in.

"So, shall I take that?" he asked, reaching out for the telesender.

"Slight problem," IQ said. "The Y2K is not completely out of the ground yet."

"And it needs to be?"

"Yes. It could still resonate."

"Oh!" George said as he finally realised. "That's what creates the ground tremors."

IQ shrugged. "Could be."

George contemplated the options; there didn't seem to be many. "So we might have to wait till they take it out tomorrow. And then seize our moment." He thought this was a good idea, but could see IQ was a tad upset. "Why don't we just go back to my place? We can then have another smoke when the effects of this one wears off. And when the time is right, I'll come in on my scooter and put the remote on the rock. That way you won't have to land. We'd just have to figure out when."

IQ ran this plan past the navcom.

We could use the girl, it suggested.

What girl? IQ asked.

"Huh?" George uttered.

The George's friend girl.

"Your girlfriend," IQ said. "Your girlfriend can tell us when the time is right."

George considered this. He let out a very slow, "Yeeeessss ..." as he thought it through.

Despite marijuana enabling them to communicate, the side effect was that he was out of his mind. And it wasn't every day he had to dream up action plans for aliens, so he was having to concentrate very hard.

Just then another voice piped up. "Hello there." The old man's voice came calling down the corridor.

George turned and saw the guy poking his head through the ship's doorway, grinning inanely. "Oh God ..." he muttered under his breath.

IQ didn't react. On the one hand, he didn't want any further interference; on the other, he was curious to find out how this scruffy individual could see the ship. "What does he want?" he asked George.

"He said, what do you ..." began George but the old man interrupted him.

"Apparently it can be used to make a bomb," he said suddenly, eyes wide with alarm. He was making his way down the corridor.

"What?" George snapped.

"The Y2K," the old man said. "That thing told me. Oh yes. And it's coming tomorrow, do you know?"

"Tell him to come in," said IQ. He went back to the flight deck.

George gestured the old man to follow.

"What do you know about Y2K?" IQ asked the old man, once they were all sitting comfortably on the flight deck.

"He said ..." George began.

"I know what he said," interrupted the old man. "That other thing told me." He had a spooked look on his face. "It's on its way, you know."

"What thing?" George demanded. "What are you on about?"

"The thing that's coming here now. It's from a far-off system – a long way away. And it's coming here again."

IQ consulted the navcom. Their competition was some way off but still heading straight for them. "How do you know this?" he asked.

"It told me," said the old man.

IQ studied the navcom, looking for an identity on this mystery party. "Who is it?" he asked.

"It's a what. It's a space probe," the old man replied.

IQ let the navcom consider this latest information.

Then he asked the old man, "Who are you?"

"My name is Madison," Madison said happily with a big grin.

"Hello, Madison," said George, holding his hand out. "My name's George and this is IQ."

He shook hands with Madison. Madison shook hands with IQ, who had finally figured out the strange custom. George and IQ were looking at Madison, both eager to know more.

"Let me explain," Madison said. "This probe comes to Earth quite often. It flies about in its flying saucer. Parks in the sky somewhere. Then the droid gets out and floats down to the ground. Floats back up, too. Oh yes. Some people think it's a weather balloon. Can you believe it? Anyway, I came across it five or six years ago down at the hospital, on the other side of the reserve. That's where I live. Oh yes. That's my home! Honest! That's where I live!" he said, grinning, as if he deserved a medal. His expression suddenly became serious. "You should see what the hospital throw out. Deary me. It's a crying shame what they put in their dumpsters. Crying shame," he said, shaking his head and gazing at the floor. "Packaging, electrical stuff, mattresses, clothing, even furniture. You'd be surprised what I can get for some of this stuff. Oh yes ..."

"There is a point to this?" George interrupted.

Madison continued, "Yes, well, there it was! Lurking around the service area at the back of the hospital."

"There was what?" George asked.

"The probe droid," replied Madison. "Floating about, collecting data, or whatever it does. I didn't know what it was, but it gave me a right going over, I can tell you. That's why I call it a probe droid." He reduced his voice to a whisper. "It probes people," he said chillingly. "And then it left Earth. Just like that! Gone! And ever since I always know when it comes back. Honest."

IQ and George were staring at Madison, but before they could respond, Madison went on. "And it's coming again. It will get here sometime tomorrow, I expect. And at some point it will come out this way." After a slight pause he suddenly blurted, "It's searching for something!" Making George jump.

"Does it know about the Y2K?" IQ asked.

Madison looked perplexed for a second. "Oh, the rock," he finally said.

Just then the proximity alarm went off.

"Let's get out of here," IQ said, turning back to the console.

"Do you know how to get back to my place?" George asked.

"We're there," said IQ, as the rustic view of George's flat corrugated-iron roof showed up on the monitor screen.

"I didn't even feel us moving! How does this thing get around?" George asked.

"The shortest route between two points is a straight line, right?" IQ said.

"Right," George replied, feeling confident that he might understand this one.

"Well, we don't go that way, takes too long," IQ explained.

George got as far as opening his mouth while waiting for the next question to get from his brain out into the open air.

"And the answer to your next question is yes," said IQ, slightly impatiently.

"Is it really?" said George. "Oh!" He covered his mouth with his hand.

"What's for dinner?" asked Madison.

Chapter 11

"So tell me more about this rock," George asked IQ as he filled the kettle.

IQ was standing in the middle of the kitchen, facing the lounge, his back to George and Madison who were lingering by the kitchen bench. George thought he'd make some herbal tea, mainly for something to do while they planned the next move. Madison sat down at the table and produced a bottle of plonk from inside his coat.

"What is that?" IQ pointed to George's old CRT TV.

"It's a secret recipe," said Madison, taking a swig.

"Huh?" said George. The reception from IQ was getting crackly. "That's a TV," he replied, once he figured what IQ was on about.

IQ tapped his head with his hand. "What was that? I think our communications are failing."

George flinched as he received more undecipherable telepathic images than clear speech. "We need to have another smoke, don't we? Hang on."

He grabbed his phone and sent a text to Steve. Then he left the kitchen and disappeared down the hallway.

IQ and Madison looked at each other as an awkward silence started to settle in.

"Do you want a drink?" Madison asked, offering the bottle to IQ, who didn't react. Madison had another go at intelligent conversation. "Is this your first time on Earth?"

IQ said nothing.

"I'm from Earth, you know," Madison said informatively.

IQ stared at him. He was a little bit lost in social interactions with non-telepathic life forms. He'd spent much of his life cooped up in his spaceship so his social skills were severely lacking. Most of his communication was done telepathically and a lot of it was pretty much automatic. Not much effort was involved in telling the navcom 'knight to B4' or 'are we there yet?'

Marijuana, however, changed all that, as he'd recently found out, and he felt it was probably easier to wait until they lit up again before resuming conversations. The strange thing was that Madison appeared to be able to understand IQ without the aid of a smoke. IQ didn't know why this was but was intrigued to find out.

"You know I ..." Madison began.

IQ interrupted. "How come you understand me without smoking that stuff?"

"I don't know," Madison replied solemnly. He thought for a few seconds. "Maybe it's something I picked up in my encounter with ... you know ..."

IQ glared at him, clearly not happy with this answer. He then went over to the TV to have a closer look.

Madison got up and began exploring the kitchen, hoping to find something to eat.

"Want a cuppa?" George asked as he came back into the room.

Madison peered over the open fridge door. "Yes please," he said.

"What does this do?" IQ called from the lounge, holding up the back panel of the TV.

"What are you doing?" George asked as he hurried over to rescue his TV from being pulled to bits.

"Why does it do this?" IQ asked, waving the back panel in the air.

George didn't know what IQ was saying. He picked up the remote and turned the TV on. "There," he said, pointing to the screen.

IQ came around to the front of the TV, but rather than looking at the screen, he snatched the remote out of George's hand. "So that's what it's for!"

"Look at the screen," said George, pointing at it. He left IQ to it.

George went back to the kitchen table, sat down and started rolling a joint. "Just help yourself, Madison," he said without looking up.

"Just feeling a bit peckish, that's all," Madison replied from behind the fridge door.

"There's bread and cheese in there. I'll be with you in a minute," George said, concentrating on the roll-up. He lit up, took a drag, got up and went over to offer it to IQ. "Here you go."

IQ poked his head up from behind the TV. He came out, took the joint and had a puff.

"Interesting?" George asked, pointing to the TV.

IQ was demolishing the joint. It was disappearing fast as he sucked it back.

"Go easy, we want it to last," George said, taking it off him.

"This," IQ said, shaking a very long finger at the TV, "is brilliant."

Strangely, even though IQ's expression never changed, George could see he was excited. "It's pretty old," he replied.

"Very simple, very brilliant. Just what I've been looking for."

George was puzzled for a moment. Then he heard rummaging coming from the kitchen. He took another puff and gave the joint back to IQ, then turned back to the kitchen. Madison was helping himself.

"Do you want it toasted, Madison?" George asked.

"Oh no," Madison replied, slapping a cheese sandwich together. He fired it at his mouth with both hands and took a massive bite. "Thush ihs fyng, thangsh," he munched at George.

Satisfied, George sat at the table. "What do you want to do now?" he asked IQ.

"I'll take this," IQ said as he held up the TV like it had no weight. He was obviously a lot stronger than the average human.

"Take it where?" asked George.

IQ thought the answer was obvious. "Crux Alumina."

George eyed IQ with suspicion. "Why?"

"It's a translayer!"

"A what?"

"This is what I've come halfway across the galaxy for!" In fact, he was in televerse communication with the navcom, which confirmed that the TV was in fact a star translayer.

"It has an electron gun," IQ said. "With a few adjustments, it will make a fine translayer."

"What's that?" George asked.

IQ quietly considered the navcom's explanation. "Communications device," he said eventually.

"Well, all right," said George reluctantly, then added, "It's half knackered anyway."

IQ grabbed the remote, then picked up the TV with it still running and carried it over to the kitchen, pulling the plug and the aerial cable out of their wall sockets in the process. He put it down on the table. "We've got to get the Y2K," he said.

Just then there was a knock at the door. George recognised the knock; it was Steve.

"Come in, dude," he called out, without thinking.

Steve swung the door open. "Hey, man, your burglar alarm's gone off." He gingerly made his way across the nail-strewn floor. "Something smells good. I brought some more," he said, holding up a bag of weed. Then he noticed George had company. "Oh ..."

What Steve did next was totally understandable, given he had never seen an alien from another planet before. Firstly, he stopped in his tracks – so far, so good. Then he stumbled back towards the door while emitting an unusual groaning noise.

George held his hand up. "Hang on, mate. These are my friends. It's all right."

Steve was at the doorway ready to bolt. "Wha-?" he managed.

"This is IQ. He's an alien from ..." He looked back at IQ. "Sorry, where are you from?"

"Sirius C Major," IQ said with tried patience.

"Oh yeah. Sirius C Major. Another planet out there somewhere. And this is Madison. He's from this planet, aren't you, Madison?"

"Oh yes," Madison replied, fairly certain. He turned to Steve. "We met."

"Huh?" Steve whimpered, all the while keeping his gaze on IQ.

"Madison was the guy who came up to us in the reserve the other day," George explained.

Steve shifted his stare to Madison and the penny dropped. "Oh, right, yes. You know him?" he asked George.

"Um, not exactly *know*. What would you say, Madison?" George asked.

"We have a lot in common," Madison said.

“Right. Well, maybe not a lot, necessarily,” George replied.

“Oh, more than you think,” Madison said, wagging half a sandwich at George.

“So wha-” Steve was trying to say something as he shifted his gaze back to IQ.

“He’s trying to say something,” said the helpful Madison.

“Yes, well, look, just sit down and we’ll tell you all about it,” George suggested.

Steve was fixated.

“Come on,” said George. “Have a seat.”

Steve slowly sat at the table but kept his eyes on IQ.

George sat down and proceeded to roll another joint. Madison had finished his sandwich and was keen to see if what George was doing involved food. He then began exploring the kitchen again when he could see that it didn’t.

“Hang on, mate, you’ll need this,” George said to Steve.

He lit up and passed the joint to Steve. Steve didn’t hesitate. He’d barely got a puff in when IQ’s two-fingered, two-thumbed hand reached across the table, homing in on the joint in Steve’s hand. Steve jumped back in his chair and dropped the joint. Quick as lightning, IQ delicately plucked it out of mid-air, before it hit the table.

“Right, we might need another,” George said calmly, glancing back at IQ, who was inhaling the joint in one go. He held out his hand to IQ and got a stub back. “Have a couple more puffs and you’ll be able to understand him,” he said to Steve.

Steve did as he was told. “Am I dreaming?” he asked.

“No, but this will help, I assure you,” George said.

“OK. If you say so.”

George figured he ought to continue with the introductions. "IQ, this is my mate Steve."

"Why?" IQ asked impassively.

"Ah, well, he just is." George gestured at his last remaining joint. "And he has plenty of this stuff to ensure we continue to understand each other."

IQ was suddenly very interested. "Hey, dude, what's it?" he said to Steve as he held out his hand.

Steve stared up at him in wide-eyed panic.

"It's all right. I taught him the custom of hand-shaking," George said.

Steve stared at the long-fingered hand and groaned some more.

"Shake, dude," said IQ, waving his hand about.

Enough cannabis was now floating around in Steve's bloodstream that he could understand that IQ was not about to rip his arm off. He timidly held out his hand and did a quick shake. "Fuckinell," he muttered. He turned to George. "You know this fella?"

"We're just helping out, aren't we, Maddy?" George said.

Madison quickly turned from the kitchen bench with a mouthful of another cheese sandwich. "Oh yesh," he said.

"You know the rock at uni?" George asked Steve.

Steve nodded.

"Well," George said as he lit the last joint, "IQ says he wants it, apparently." He shrugged.

IQ made a growling noise.

George corrected himself. "Like, *needs* it. To run his spaceship." He looked up at IQ. "That right?"

"Yes," IQ replied.

"So we have to figure out how to get it without anyone seeing us," George explained.

"What the fuck are you talking about?" Steve asked.

George explained the whole story to Steve, including how he'd lost his laptop, then recovered it.

At one point Madison chipped in with, "It's coming, you know." But George ignored him.

"Well, they're taking that rock out, eh," Steve said, once George had finished.

"Yeah, they've moved a crane in and it looks like they might remove it sometime. Maybe tomorrow," said George.

"No, they're taking it out now," said Steve.

"Really? Now? At night?" George turned to IQ. "They're taking it out now. Do you want to have a look?"

"Let's go," said IQ. He grabbed the TV, strode towards the door, then turned back and pointed at Steve's bag of weed. "Bring that."

"Yeah, hang on," called George as he began to gather his bits.

"Where are you going?" Steve asked.

George grabbed his satchel from the table and shoved the bag of weed inside. "Come on. If nothing else, you can have a ride on his spaceship. It's really cool. Come on, Maddy."

Madison held up a sandwich-filled hand. "Righto!"

Chapter 12

Once they were seated on the flight deck, IQ brought the university courtyard up on the screen.

"You can monitor it from here?" Steve asked.

"We *are* here," said George, glancing out the window. "This thing moves."

They surveyed the scene below. The workmen had erected lights, cleared the barriers, backed a truck up and a crane was ready to haul the rock out of the ground.

"Can't we just bowl on in?" asked Steve. "Those guys will freak and take off when they see this fella."

"Trouble is, we can't land here. And we have to land to get out," said George. "The nearest clear landing place is in the reserve."

"If we can hijack that truck, we could drive it down to the reserve," said Steve.

"Can you drive a truck?" George asked.

"Dunno. Can't be too hard."

"There's no road down there anyway."

"Maybe we should land and the three of us come over to the worksite?" suggested Madison.

"Then what?" George asked. "'Scuse me, can we have that rock please, mister? And can you help us haul it back to a waiting spaceship?"

They were silent for a few seconds, then Steve murmured to George, "What is IQ exactly?"

IQ looked at him.

"What do you mean?" George asked.

"Well, you know, we're humans from planet Earth. What sort of, ah, animal, thing, is he?"

Madison was quick to answer. "He's a rev."

"A what?" asked George.

"A rev," Madison repeated. "Isn't that right?"

"Yes," IQ confirmed. "Revision 3, to be precise. We populate the three planets orbiting Sirius C. Ten light-years away."

George thought he could detect a hint of homesickness in IQ. "Do you have a family?"

"No, not like humans. We are quite solitary."

After an awkward pause, Steve asked softly, "So what do we do?"

IQ had been going over things with the navcom. "Yes, we can land and then someone needs to put the telesender on or near the Y2K."

"I'll do it," said George. "Take us down."

In no time at all they had landed in the reserve. IQ handed a large steel lifting shackle to George. It was surprisingly light. "I'll take the ship back up over the site so I can monitor you."

"What am I supposed to do with this?" George asked.

"It's the telesender. It's copied the form of an inconspicuous object down there," IQ explained. "Looks like they're using a few of them. Just put it as close to the rock as you can. On it, would be better."

"It might fall off. Got any Blu Tack?"

"I got chewing gum," said Steve.

"That'll do. Right, let's go."

“I’ll come too,” said Madison. “You might need someone with experience.”

Steve shot a puzzling glare at Madison. “Experience?”

“Oh yes,” Madison replied, completely seriously. “I was probed, you know.”

“Wha-?”

“Yep, Maddy’s our resident UFO expert,” George said as they descended the ramp.

“You’re kidding,” said Steve.

“Oh no,” said Madison. “And it’s coming again. Tomorrow.”

“What’s coming?” Steve asked.

“The probe droid.”

“The what?”

“Space probe droid,” Madison said, as if it were obvious.

“From where?”

“You know the Southern Cross?” said Madison.

“Yeah.”

“There.”

Steve frowned as he thought about this. He was walking behind George who took the lead. “Jeez you guys talk a lot of shit,” he said eventually.

They were making their way up the dimly lit path from the reserve to the university. They got to the edge of the courtyard and positioned themselves a behind a raised garden bordering a seating area. From there, they could observe the worksite and plan their next move. The workmen were fitting lifting straps around the rock.

“Man, that thing’s freaky,” said Steve, under his breath.

“What is?” asked George.

“That IQ.”

“Yeah, he’s a funny guy.”

“We should ask him stuff,” Steve suggested.

"Like what?"

"I don't know. How does a spaceship work?"

"Yeah, that'd be a doozy," George replied. "We could sure show NASA a thing or two."

"Yeah, man, that would be unbelievable," Steve said, realising all sorts of opportunities. He surveyed the scene. "So, what do we do now?"

"I think we'll have to get round the other side of the courtyard," said George. "We could come through the garden behind that truck."

"You'll have to be careful not to stand on anyone," offered Madison.

Yet another random comment from Madison, George thought. "What?"

"People sleep in that garden," Madison explained, matter-of-factly. "When it's not raining."

"Yeah, right!" Steve said sceptically.

Madison shrugged. "Well, just saying."

"OK, we'll have to keep an eye out," George said. "Don't want anyone giving our position away. But once we're on the other side of the truck, we'll be out of sight."

"Outta sight, man," Steve said, hippy-like. "But what happens if it telesends the truck into his spaceship? That could get nasty."

"I think his telesend system is a bit more sophisticated than that," George replied. "You got some gum?"

"Oh right." Steve rummaged in his pocket and handed a stick to George.

"Ah lovely," said Madison and held out his hand. Steve dropped a stick of gum into Madison's hand which he then pocketed.

They watched the workmen for a few quiet seconds, waiting for their moment.

"Hi, George!" Charley suddenly announced rather

breezily out of nowhere.

"Christ!" George cried. If there was a roof, he would nearly have hit it. They all turned to see Charley standing behind them.

"Jeez, Charley, what're you doing here?" George asked.

"I've just come out of my Taekwondo class."

"Yeah?" said Steve, highly impressed.

"What are you doing?" she asked.

"Oh nothing," said George, hoping that would suffice.

"Well, my dear," said the very discreet Madison, "we're trying to put a telesender onto that rock over there without being seen."

"Oh, are they taking it away?" Charley asked.

"Looks like it," said George.

"Where to?"

"Don't know."

"I thought it was going up to the lab," she said.

George thought about this. "Then why would they do that at night?"

"Good question. We're studying it in our geology class. Dr Segway says it's very special."

"Dr Segway?"

"My geology lecturer."

"So what are these guys doing then?" George said, surveying the scene.

"Dunno," Charley replied. "I can call Dr Segway and ask him."

"You got his number?" George asked. "Yeah, do it."

She dug her phone out of her bag. "Hi, it's Charlene Dibble from geology stage three. Hi. Dr Segway, you know that rock out in the courtyard? Yeah ... well they're taking it away ... right now ... dunno, some workmen ... dunno ... oh, I just came out of Taekwondo and bumped into some friends here, we're just talking about it ... the seating area at the far end of the main block ... OK, bye." She put the phone away. "He says he'll be 20 minutes." She walked passed George and out into the courtyard.

"You off?" George called after her.

Charley kept walking towards the worksite. They watched her go right up and start talking to the workmen.

"What's she doing?" asked Steve.

Just then, there was the sound of someone cleaning their teeth. George and Steve turned to see Madison doing just that.

Meanwhile, IQ was observing all this from 100 metres above the courtyard, totally unseen, of course.

While Charley was arguing with the workmen, George made his move. "OK. You go back Charley up," he said, tapping Steve on the shoulder. "And me and Maddy will go round the other side of the truck."

"Right," said Steve and quickly walked over to the worksite.

The foreman was getting frustrated with Charley's persistence. "Look, I'm sorry, but this is a worksite, there are safety protocols."

Charley argued, "Well I just think it all looks a bit suspicious, when we're told the rock must stay there and we're studying it and everything and here you are taking it away in the middle of the night. What do you expect people to think?"

"What's happening?" Steve enquired as he approached.

"They think they've got authority to take the rock away, but I don't believe them," she said. "In fact, I think we should call the police."

"You want authority?" replied the foreman. "One minute." He walked briskly over to his pickup truck.

"Who are these guys?" Steve asked Charley under his breath.

"They're just contractors, but I don't know who they're working for," she murmured.

The foreman came back with a piece of paper. "Here you go," he said and showed the paper to her without letting it go.

"This is a purchase order from the Department of Scientific Research," she said.

"That's right," said the foreman.

"But it's blank," she argued. "There's no instruction or anything. What do you take me for?"

"Look, if you want to make a big deal of this, by all means, call someone, but we're carrying on. Please stay back, or I'm going to be the one who calls the police," the foreman insisted.

Just then, they were lit up by a pair of headlights from Dr Segway's vehicle as it turned into the courtyard driveway.

"Charlene. What's happening?" he said as he got out of his car.

"I thought this rock was going up to the lab," she said.

"My understanding is that it's been commandeered by the Department of Scientific Research. This happened late this afternoon, although I didn't think they'd move it now. But there are concerns that it could be dangerous," he said. "How's it going, lads?" He waved to the workmen who mumbled their various replies.

"Dangerous?" Charley asked. "In what way?"

"It emits some kind of electromagnetic radiation, most unusual. There could be side effects if one stands too close for too long," he said. The workmen quietly shuffled back from the rock. "They made the order this afternoon to get it moved to a safer facility so it can be studied further."

"So the university can study it further?" Charley asked.

"Hopefully. I'm working on a research exchange plan with the centre."

While Charley was keeping the workmen distracted George and Madison skirted around the back of the main block, then double-backed through the garden to the other side of the truck. They crouched in the bushes for a bit while George surveyed the scene. He handed the telesender to Madison. "Hold this for a sec," he said as he adjusted his position.

The truck was parked fairly close to the garden, so they just had to pick their moment when the workmen were not looking their way. Between the garden and the truck there were piles of assorted materials and equipment stacked on the asphalt, and George just had to make sure he didn't trip over anything when he made his way to the truck.

He could see Charley was doing a great job keeping the workmen preoccupied and just as he whispered, "Let's go," Madison tripped over his own feet and dropped the telesender.

He quickly recovered and went to pick it up but realised there were a number of identical shackles lying around on the ground in front of him. He picked up one of them, hesitated, then picked up another. Fortunately, the ambient noise from the site and passing traffic had masked his fumble.

George was a few paces ahead, and half turning, whispered, "Shh ..." He reached his hand back. "Hand me the telesender."

Madison looked at each of the two shackles he was holding, did a quick mental eeny-meeny-miny-moe and handed one of them to George and pocketed the other in his trench coat.

George then reached over the truck deck and tucked the telesender under the rock. Satisfied that the gum held it in place adequately, he quietly retreated to the waiting Madison who promptly fell head first into the begonias.

George gave Madison a scornful look. "Let's get out of here," he said and took the lead back around the main block.

Charley and Steve wandered back across the courtyard and joined them a few minutes later.

"Any luck?" Steve asked, rather apprehensively as he noticed bits of begonia through Madison's beard.

"Yep," said George. "IQ can telesend when he's ready. Let's go back to the reserve."

"Right," said Steve.

As they moved out, Charley gave George a puzzled look. "What do you mean – telesend?"

Chapter 13

The gang of four, led by George, with Charley close behind, marched up the ramp into IQ's ship. Once Charley had got over her initial shock, they lit up so they could hold a meaningful conversation. Surprisingly, Charley quickly adapted to the situation and took a keen interest in recovering the rock.

"Have you telesent yet?" George asked IQ.

"Something's not right," IQ replied. "You definitely got the telesender on or near the Y2K?"

"Yep, it's directly under it."

They watched the truck drive out of the courtyard and down the street, followed by Dr Segway's car. The monitor zoomed in on the rock, strapped to the deck of the truck.

"Right, here goes," IQ said and activated the telesender.

Madison vanished. Everyone jumped, except IQ.

"Shit!" said Steve. "Where's Madison?"

IQ put his head in his hands. "I knew it!" he groaned.

"Has he been telesent?" George asked. "Where is he?"

"He's in the transfer bay," said an exasperated IQ. "This way."

He wearily got out of his seat and went out the door. He led the team to a door at the far end of the corridor.

The door opened to a small, featureless room, lined with what looked like stainless steel. Standing right in the middle was a rather stunned-looking Madison.

"Are you all right?" Charley asked.

Madison didn't respond. He stood there with his eyes wide and his mouth open, like he'd just had an electric shock. IQ did a quick search of Madison's trench coat and found the telesender. He said something the others couldn't interpret.

"Come on," Charley said, guiding Madison out into the corridor. "Come and sit down." She turned to IQ. "Will he be all right?"

IQ, unconcerned, groaned, shrugged his shoulders and shook his head.

They ushered Madison back to the flight deck with IQ trailing dejectedly.

Rev telesending technology had been around for many years and had evolved into various types. The proximity type was the most reliable but could be inconvenient to have to get the telesender near or onto the object you want to telesend. Basically, the telesender analysed the object you wanted to send and anything attached to it. It could determine what is the object and what is not. That avoided any mix-ups when, say, a fly got in the way; the telesender would know to leave the fly behind. That is basic telesend theory 101.

Something that is not generally done is telesending a living being. Theoretically it's possible, as Madison just found out, but there are also risks. The unfortunate thing was, in order to determine the dangers, they actually had to try it, and early trials of telesender prototypes were in fact designed to telesend living beings. Half the time it worked fine, but occasionally the subject would suffer nausea or drowsiness, or have an extra arm. But the most common effects from being telesent were mood swings, headaches and general bitchiness, which would typically last a few days. They labelled this Post Materialisation Syndrome or PMS, and it was so unbearable for everyone else that no one could really put up with it. So PMS was outlawed, which was by far the most sensible thing to do.

Luckily, Madison soon came right, with no ill effects, or at least, none more so than usual. The first thing he did after sitting down was to rummage around in his coat pocket and get his toothbrush out.

Follow that truck, IQ firmly instructed the navcom.

We have no more residual power. We'll have to wait till tomorrow so we can draw on solar energy.

That was not what IQ wanted to hear. He closed his eyes and fumed for a second.

George thought something was up. "You all right?"

"We've run out of power," IQ said calmly, but with the potential to explode. "We have no fuel, we have no residual power. We'll have to wait till tomorrow to draw energy from the sun."

Although he didn't really show it, IQ was extremely upset. There was a certain tension in the air that the others could feel. Except for Madison; he was lost in his own little world.

Finally, Charley broke the silence. "You need the rock to power this?"

"Yep," George replied.

"Would a little bit be any good?" she asked.

"What do you mean?"

She rummaged through her bag and pulled out the vial. She prised off the cap, removed some cotton wool and tipped the rock fragment out.

IQ's eyes lit up.

She held out her hand. "Would this be any good?"

All stared at her hand.

"Is that a bit of it?" George asked.

"Yep," Charley replied. "It was all I could break off."

IQ's stare suddenly switched from her hand to her face. "You were lucky it didn't explode," he said. "Splitting this material must be done under highly controlled conditions." He held out his hand. "May I?"

"Take it," she said.

IQ delicately took the fragment between a finger and thumb. He moved off his seat and headed out the door.

The others sat quietly for a minute. Especially Madison, who was still in his own little world.

IQ returned and sat in his seat and silently conferred with the navcom. Eventually he said, "We have power." He seemed more sober than elated.

"Great," said George. "What do we do now?"

"We follow that vehicle."

It didn't take long for the spaceship to catch up with the truck. The group watched proceedings on the screen, as the ship silently hovered a few hundred metres up in the night air.

The truck waited at the main gate of the government-owned research facility. Once it got clearance, it was driven through an open roller door in the largest building on the site. A few minutes later it re-emerged, minus the rock, and left the site. Dr Segway, who observed the delivery from his car across the street, then moved off.

The site was well protected with an electrified security fence around its perimeter, electronic access control on the gate and doors and video surveillance. Luckily there was no protection in place to prevent the infiltration of spaceships from above.

"Now what do we do?" said George as they surveyed the scene on the monitor screen.

IQ glanced at George with an expression of 'I wish you'd stop saying that'.

"Well," Charley piped up. "According to Dr Segway, we should be visiting this place to do further tests on the rock."

"When will that be?" George asked.

"Not sure. Hopefully next week."

"Tests?" said IQ. "I can give you all the data you'd ever want about Y2K," he said, eyes fixed on the monitor.

"Hey, yeah," Steve said to Charley. "You'd get top of the class."

"Do you have a name for it?" Charley asked IQ.

"Y2K," he replied. "It's an antigravite ore, most likely originating from the Fleurius region."

"Is that where you're from?" Steve asked.

"No," IQ replied simply.

"No, he's from Sirius," said George.

"Y2K?" Charley wondered out loud. "That's like Y2K. You know – year two thousand."

George and Steve looked at each other. "Oh yeah!" they said in unison as they finally realised.

"Is it very rare?" Charley asked IQ.

"It's the only detectable piece in this part of the galaxy," IQ said. "There's plenty of it on Fleurius 12 but there's a miners' strike at the moment." He gave Charley a stern look. "It's highly dangerous and needs to be handled with care."

"Couldn't you have just waited till the strike was over?" asked Steve.

"If you felt like waiting centuries, yes," he said.

"How do you mean, dangerous?" Charley asked. "Is it radioactive?"

"Partly radioactive, partly resonant. It has multiple energy bands that correspond to different frequencies. It will have a primary resonant frequency that will produce maximum energy output. Refining its radioactive isotopes greatly increases energy levels. The process of harnessing this energy is called partial particle accela-tronics. This is done at normal temperatures, and it means if you knock it and the vibration happens to be on or close to its resonant frequency, it could explode."

"And we don't want that," George said helpfully.

IQ looked at him impassively. "No, we don't want that," he said firmly. "The unique thing about this element is that it remains intact after energy release. Ready to be used again."

"Like a battery that never loses charge," said Steve.

"Exactly," IQ replied.

Steve grinned, chuffed he'd joined in the science banter.

"Wow, that sounds amazing," said Charley. "So what could we use it for on Earth?"

IQ shrugged. "A piece this size will power a city for centuries." He paused for effect. "You could also make a truly horrifying and devastating weapon."

There was silence for a few seconds.

"What sort of weapon?" George asked.

"A truly horrifying and devastating one," IQ replied. "And from what I understand about human behaviour and the social and political history here, it would not take you long to find that out, and my bet is that will be precisely what you would use it for."

Another silent pause as the team took this in. They all realised he was right. That would be *precisely* what they'd use it for.

"Isn't that what happens, you know, where it comes from?" George asked.

"No," IQ said simply.

George recoiled. "But surely you have power-hungry tyrants, super-political dictators, terrorists and general mad-arsed radicals who would get this stuff to make weapons?"

"No, we don't," IQ said in all seriousness. "Not in the Sirius system and certainly not in the Fleurius system. It has been the main energy source in that part of the galaxy for many millennia. Although it has recently been superseded by synthlight wavetable technology, which is still quite expensive at the moment."

"And you couldn't just go to the mining place to get some?" Charley asked.

"No. It's currently off limits. There are huge security protocols in the industry anyway."

"So it's come all this way. Halfway across the galaxy," George pondered.

"A lot less than half, but, yes," said IQ. "A long time ago."

"Way before the city was established here, presumably," George suggested.

"If the city was here, it would have got flattened on impact," IQ said to George in the driest way possible. He turned to the group. "How do we get in?"

"Well, like I said, we might have a field trip there," said Charley. "I'll ask Dr Segway tomorrow."

"Right," George said. "Then all we have to do is get the telesender to it."

"Yes," said IQ. "I'll park here in the meantime."

Amazingly, they were in the reserve again.

"Shit, we're back!" said Steve, looking out the window. "How does this thing move?"

"You know the distance between two points?" George began, then immediately trailed off as he realised he was way out of his depth.

"Huh?" Steve asked. "What two points?"

"Ah ..." George desperately gathered his thoughts before he was interrupted.

"Oh!" Madison suddenly came to life. "You mean cyclotronic geo-magnetics! The interpolation of geometrically opposed dipole transference."

Everyone looked at him.

"What?" George demanded.

Madison shrugged. "You know – relative gravitational momentum using the evolving harmonics in the Earth's magnetic field as a time-referenced geo-guidance network."

There was a brief, dumbstruck silence.

"What are you on about?" Charley asked.

"He's on the right track," IQ said casually, without breaking his gaze from the monitor screen. "Though I can't claim to know the ins and outs of the ship's cyclotronics system; the navcom handles that."

"How do you know this?" George asked Madison.

"That thing told me," Madison said, pointing to the console.

"The navcom?" George asked.

"Yes." Madison looked around as if it were obvious.

George was quite exasperated. "So how can you do that, when *we* need to get stoned out of our heads to be able to talk to IQ?"

Madison bowed his head solemnly. "Well, it's like I told you. I got probed," he said quietly. He looked up. The others were giving him confused looks. "Remember the space probe I was telling you about?"

George, Charley and Steve all replied at the same time.

"Yeah."

"No."

"Huh?"

"Well, the first time I met it, it, I don't know," he sighed. Suddenly he looked spooked. "It probed my mind. Honest!"

George was sceptical. "It probed your mind?"

"Yes!"

"You say the *first* time," Charley asked. "How many times have you met it?

"Oh, several. It comes every year. It knows where I live." He gazed at the floor and took his hat off. He almost looked like he was about to cry. He was still holding on to his toothbrush.

Charley reached over and sympathetically patted his arm. "Aw ..."

Steve broke from his gormless expression. "So that explains it then," he said, somewhat baffled, and hoping someone would say what was going on in syllables he could comprehend.

IQ was observing this group discussion with great patience, and he was keen to move things along. "We need to return to the site with a plan to get in as soon as possible."

"Right," said Charley, quickly returning to the situation at hand. "I'll try and find out tomorrow when we're going to visit the research complex. How can I get back to you? Do you have a phone?"

"Just get back to the cerebral one," IQ said, indicating George.

"Huh?" George piped up. "George, the name's George."

"Right."

"But how will we contact you?" Charley asked.

"Come back to this point to report," IQ said as he indicated the landing spot in the reserve that was up on the screen. "You'll be able to see my ship and I will know you are here," he said, and then added rather sternly, "Let's keep this between the four of us, OK?"

"OK," everyone agreed and began making moves to disembark.

Once they were back on solid ground, Madison went off on his own, babbling something or other about being disassembled and reassembled and checking his pockets in case anything was missing. He wandered back to his digs – a disused generator room, relatively out of sight, around the back of the hospital utility block.

Madison's little home was ideal. In fact, it was complete luxury, for homeless accommodation. It was a large concrete room that once housed the hospital's backup generator. As the hospital expanded over time, a new generator room was built at the other end of the block, and when Madison found the old room, the redundant generator had long been removed and the place was filled with various bits of old machinery, furniture and building materials. Madison moved in and did the hospital a favour by gradually selling off the room's contents on eBay.

Luckily, the hospital staff had forgotten about the room, as they had plenty of much more important rooms to go into.

Meanwhile, George, Charley and Steve quietly made their way through the bush in the darkness up towards the university's main block.

George broke the silence. "Was he taking the piss calling me cerebral?"

Steve laughed. "Yeah, mate. I think he's got a sense of humour."

Charley gave George a friendly pat on the back. "You're the man," she said, smiling up at him.

George caught the sparkle in her eyes and felt a zing of affection surge through him. He smiled at her shyly. It's funny, he thought; he could converse with Charley on intellectual subjects or problem-solving difficult aliens and be quite rational, even under the influence of cannabis, but her simple gesture and lovely smile suddenly rendered him completely, stupidly love-struck. He was also glad Steve was walking in front so his little moment with Charley remained private.

It was now approaching midnight and the university gates were locked so they had to follow the perimeter fence to the street and then double-back to the car park. By the time they got there, they'd sobered up and reality began sinking in.

George suddenly realised, "Hey, I've got no wheels."

"Ah, me neither," said Steve.

"I can give you a lift," Charley said. "The car's just over here."

"Cool," said Steve. "Just back to George's place, if that's OK."

"Yep, no problem," she said.

"You're not still tripping?" George asked her.

"I feel fine. I didn't actually inhale, you know."

The other two looked at her inquisitively.

"I think you only need a tiny amount of whatever is in cannabis to be able to understand IQ," she said. "At least, that's what happened with me. Madison didn't smoke any."

"Oh yeah, Madison," said George. "What are the chances of coming across someone who can understand alien-speak right when you meet an alien?"

"Well, there you go," said Steve. "He has his uses."

"Yeah, alien translator," George replied. "He'll make a mint if we ever go intergalactic."

There were only a few vehicles left in the car park and Charley led them over to her Nissan Leaf.

"Hey, this is pretty cool," said Steve. "Electric, is it?"

"Yep," Charley replied as they all clambered in. "Actually, it's not mine; I couldn't afford anything like this. It's my brother's – he's overseas at the moment. He said I could use it. And I really like it. I mean, I firmly believe we need to end our dependency on fossil fuels. Don't you think?"

George chipped in, "You know the manufacture and disposal of batteries has a relatively high carbon footprint process. And the generation of electricity to charge the things is often sourced from fossil-fuelled power stations," he said, and then immediately wished he hadn't. He had no intention of putting Charley's ideals down, particularly as they seemed to be warming to each other.

"Oh yes, I know," she replied. "But we have to start somewhere. And I believe the technology will evolve rapidly and carbon footprints will reduce once people start using it. Your place, George?"

"Yep. Thirty-two Constellation Crescent, planet Earth."

"Hey, maybe IQ could give us some tips on emission-free transportation," Steve remarked.

"You know, that's not a silly idea," said George. "I wonder if he can enlighten us on his technology."

"Well, I tell you mate," said Steve, "if you introduced a spaceship like IQ's to the world, it would be, like, I don't know, the invention of the wheel, or something."

"Absolutely. It would be huge," George agreed. "I don't know how his spaceship runs, although it seems Madison does. And it appears to be emissions free. What do you think, Charley?"

"Maybe IQ's technology is too advanced for us. We might not understand it. Or it might need materials we don't have on Earth. Like Y2K for a start."

"Do you have any more of that?" George asked.

“No, that was the only bit I could break off,” she said. “It was insane. So hard. Funnily enough, when that bit came off, I didn’t actually hit it that hard. Like it was on just the right spot. Hopefully we’ll find out more when we visit the research centre.”

By the time they got to George’s place the conversation had died down a bit.

“You guys wanna come in for a smoke or a cup of tea or talk about aliens?” George offered.

“No, I’ve had enough of smoke for one night,” Charley replied.

“I know what you mean,” said Steve. “You have to really concentrate on what’s going on, but you’re out of your brain. Not easy.”

“And if we have to do much more of this, we’ll have to find Madison’s secret,” said George.

“OK, I’ll head off,” said Charley. “Mineralogy at 9.30 tomorrow. That’s early enough for a student.”

“Yep. Call it a night, eh,” said Steve as he got out of the car. “Band practice tomorrow night, right?” he said to George who had also got out.

“Sure,” he said. He bent down to the open passenger window. “Bye, Charley. Thanks for your help on this.”

“Oh that’s all right. Quite exciting really,” she said with a smile.

There was that smile again, George thought. “See you later,” he said and set off down the driveway.

Chapter 14

George woke with a start. He'd heard something. A bump in the night. One of those bumps that seems to echo around your head for a while as if it was trying to make a point. And it had all the dreary acoustic characteristics of coming from his kitchen.

It wasn't an everyday bump. It was one of those bumps normally associated with some kind of blood-sucking, brain-eating zombie-like vampire monster alien, or whatever overactive imaginations can conjure up in the middle of the night. You couldn't see it, but it could see you. It was going to get you. Just like in the movies.

He lay there listening, wondering if he'd dreamt it. He couldn't remember dreaming. He was sure it was a non-dream bump.

The night was very quiet, apart from the single rogue bump. And apart from the rhythmic thumping of his heartbeat in his ears, it was dead quiet; too quiet. No other sound that he could make a reference to in order to gauge how loud or soft the noise was, but as far as he was concerned, or at least his imagination was concerned, against the backdrop of total silence, it was loud enough. It was loud enough to be a killer sound. It was still faintly resonating in his head, replaying over and over, reminding him that the situation was far from being resolved.

His bedroom was lit slightly by the ambient streetlight glow. It had that darkened-contrast, black-and-white look to it where it was difficult to see detail and all too easy to interpret shapes of things into shapes of other things.

He looked at his bedside clock. 2.27. Is that all? Couldn't it have been more like 5.27? Something close to morning? So he could conceivably be saved by the reassuring break of dawn? Typical, he thought. How come all the scary things happen in the dead of night?

There was the sound of something heavy dragging on the kitchen floor. A rush of blood hit George's head as his pulse went into overdrive. For a few seconds he lay there, not daring to move, straining to hear more. Anything to verify that this was indeed a real nightmare situation and that he might have to do something about it at some point: either run screaming half-naked down the hallway, or hide under the covers. What was it going to be? He had to find out. He would investigate; that's what he would do.

He sat up slowly, quietly as he could, and swung his feet onto the floor. He stood up and pulled a stupid face as the floorboard creaked.

He went for the main light switch by the door. No, he thought, switching the light on would compromise his position. He'd be lit up like a Christmas tree and half blinded while his eyes made their adjustment.

He opened the top drawer of the tallboy, took out a flashlight and turned it on. Much to his surprise, it worked. He crept slowly to the door, picked up his left shoe on the way and brandished it in his left hand. Where's a baseball bat when you need one? Or a gun? Yeah, an AK47; that's what he needed. One with a flashlight mounted on it and laser-aiming and an endless magazine of bullets. Also a pair of thermal imaging goggles would be good. How come he didn't have one of those handy? They'd be perfect for occasions like this.

He proceeded slowly down the hallway, shining the flashlight around randomly as he went. He reached the kitchen within a few paces, groped round the doorway and pressed the light switch. Nothing. *No light.* This had all the hallmarks of your everyday, classic nightmare. But he knew it was worse, much worse, because this was real life. You didn't feel this bad in a nightmare. You didn't feel the bare floorboards under your feet or smell stale joint smoke or notice the cold night air when you're in a nightmare. You tend to notice other things – like blood-sucking, brain-eating zombie-like vampire monster aliens coming to get you. No, this was too real. The darkness was too real. The adrenaline was too real. The probe droid sitting in the middle of the kitchen was too real.

In fact, George didn't know what the droid looked like and had taken Madison's explanation of it with a grain of salt. The rational parts of his brain assumed the thing currently floating a few inches above his kitchen floor was something to do with IQ and that all would become clear following the relevant communication with him later in the day.

Unfortunately, the signals from the rational parts of his brain were completely overshadowed by the signals from his scared-out-of-your-wits part of his brain and they were signalling him to pull a stupid face, leap into the air and yell out any old random thing. George did this rather well. He also dropped the flashlight, threw the shoe out the open back door and stumbled heavily against the hall doorway.

In the darkness, the droid looked a bit like an upside-down Coke bottle with various small appendages sticking out the base and around the midriff. It was about a metre and a half high. Its flattened head was the widest part and could swivel. It had a small disk on the side of the head that let off a faint blue glow – presumably its eye. Various antennae-looking bits stuck up on top. There was also a faint red glow about its midriff.

The thing moved across the floor towards George. It was actually quite a graceful movement. The various appendages folded or unfolded themselves, telescoped in or out, looking something like automated robotic surgical instruments. As it moved, one of the larger appendages dragged on the floor briefly, before folding itself up. This was the sound George had heard a few minutes before.

The back door was open and presumably the mechanical creature had deactivated George's can-of-nails burglar alarm as he didn't hear it go off and it certainly would have created a far louder noise than a bump in the night.

George scrambled into the living room and established a defensive position behind the couch. Ideally, he wanted to reach for the phone, but it was in the kitchen. And his mobile was in his satchel on the kitchen table. While he was contemplating phoning backup of some kind, his brain received some vague information about what the droid was and what it was doing.

George got a vibe. That's probably the best way he could describe it; a curious feeling that his mind interpreted into some kind of message. The vibe he got was that the droid's mission was to track the Y2K and it meant no harm. The data it had gathered from its previous visits and more recent activities had led it to George's flat and it was just having a look around, if that's OK, thank you very much.

"Wh-what do you want?" George blurted out.

The droid didn't answer. It silently floated over towards him, to where the TV used to be, constantly taking in information on everything as it went.

George scrambled around the couch, back into the kitchen, picked up the flashlight and shone it on the droid. It looked even more frightening with bits of it lit up. George could see detail of the thing – flanges, wires, manifolds, gudgeons, shiny bits. It reminded George of the insides of his scooter, but obviously more hi-tech; his scooter had trouble starting, let alone floating about the place. He couldn't imagine it moving so gracefully, no matter how many attractive mirrors he added to it.

The droid didn't seem to mind this cross-examination at all. It followed George as he backed off into the hallway. It then floated past him and out the back door. As soon as it crossed the threshold to the deck, George's can of nails came crashing to the floor, the kitchen light came on and the refrigerator hummed into life.

George yelped as nails flew everywhere, and cowered down by the hall doorway. The droid paused on the back deck briefly. George adjusted his cower into a strategic defensive position, ready to bolt down the hall and leap into bed should such an action be necessary. But he bravely stood his ground, or rather, squatted, and shone the flashlight on the thing.

The droid sent out one last message – a terrible warning of something totally catastrophic. It then floated down into the long grass of the backyard over to where the marijuana plants were, circled around them, paused, and then floated off. It quickly gathered speed and disappeared up into the night sky.

George spent the rest of the night wide awake.

Chapter 15

The next day Charley was in the mineralogy stage two lecture, and up for group discussion was the data they'd gathered from the mysterious rock. So far, there was more or less unanimous agreement that the rock had come from outer space and that it was very different to any other mineral on Earth.

However, their data was confusing. It was almost as if the rock changed its properties on a daily basis. Readings on magnetism, density, crystal structure, thermal conductance and resistivity and a host of other attributes seemed to change randomly. Graphs of some of these were up on the projector screen in front of the class, and there didn't seem to be any pattern to them.

Dr Segway was leading the review. "We've discussed crystal structure and hardness, and in these terms, we can loosely conclude that it's a similar material to pure quartz, with the hardness of diamond – probably harder. However, its thermal and insulating properties seem to go right against that idea."

Up to now, Charley hadn't shown Dr Segway her discovery of the mysterious mist swirling around inside the small piece of Black Star she'd chipped off. She was intending to share her discovery at some point, but for now she desperately hoped the chip remained under the radar while it powered IQ's spaceship.

She looked down at her notes and noticed the heading Black Star. She thought about George's dream and his 'Black Star' tune. Maybe it was an amazing coincidence. Maybe the rock had some weird power that aligned people's thoughts.

She reminisced fondly about their evening in the Irish bar and their hilarious stagger back to the university afterwards.

Her daydream was interrupted by the door to the lecture theatre opening. The Geology Course Director, Professor Hal Dawson, poked his head in and motioned for Dr Segway.

"One moment," Dr Segway said to the class and signalled to one of the students, who was operating the data show. "Martin, can you put up the next set of results?"

"Sorry to interrupt," the professor said under his breath, when Dr Segway got to the door. "We're in a bit of a political football match with the scientific research government department and, believe it or not, the SIS. It appears there's great international interest in this rock and it may become a security issue. They've asked us to cease further studying and discussion about it and to keep it hush-hush. There's an agent from the SIS waiting in my office to see you when you've finished here." The professor smiled sympathetically. "Sorry," he said, and backed out.

"OK, thanks," Dr Segway replied. Somewhat mystified, he returned his attention to the class. "Right, we'd better get on and discuss this week's sandstone lab, before we run out of time. Martin, can you close that please and bring up the lab brief? Why would we want to bombard sandstone with X-rays? Anyone?"

Later that morning, Dr Segway made his way to Professor Dawson's office to see what all the fuss was about. The professor was always welcoming to visitors, staff and students alike, and Dr Segway enjoyed his company – he was smart and articulate, always dressed formally when at university, but he had a casual, easy-going demeanour, and a knack of putting people at ease.

"Ah, Brian, come in. This is Roger Mora, Foreign Liaison Officer of the Security Intelligence Service."

"Sounds like a fancy name for secret agent," Dr Segway said jokingly.

Roger Mora laughed. "Well ..." He put his cup of tea down, stood up and they exchanged greetings.

The professor continued, "And Roger, this is Dr Brian Segway, senior lecturer in geology and mineralogy. We were just talking about our rock. Seems we're going to have to put it in the capable hands of the American Nuclear Society."

"Really?" Dr Segway replied. "They know what it is, do they?"

The professor laughed. "They're not giving too much away there, but they want to analyse it further, stateside. So I'm afraid we're losing it."

"I see," Dr Segway said, looking slightly miffed.

Roger then said, "Yes, the rock contains a highly unstable element and could be dangerous, according to the Americans. And it's gone to the top. We've received instruction from the Prime Minister to cooperate with them. So it's quite a big deal. There's a nuclear scientist by the name of John Davies, from San Fernando University on his way here now to oversee the transfer back to Los Alamos. We've also been instructed to keep this quiet. So it's currently in the DSR facility over in Avondale, where

Mr Davies can have a closer look and maybe do a few tests or whatever, and then arrange for the shipment to New Mexico."

Professor Dawson added, "The Department of Scientific Research are also sweeping the area again. You'll see them around campus. The word is they're carrying out a city-wide survey, in fact."

"Good luck to them," Dr Segway said, clearly annoyed. "So do you want me to do anything?"

"Just keeping you informed for now," the professor said. "But you'll meet Mr Davies tomorrow and hopefully we can set up a research exchange thing with them; they're interested in the data we've collected so far."

"I'm meeting him at the airport," Roger explained. "And I'll be in touch."

"And we can then arrange a field trip for the students?" Dr Segway suggested.

"We'll discuss that tomorrow," Roger said with a non-committal smile.

Later in the geology lab, Charley and her lab partner, Sue, were carrying out all sorts of complex radiography experiments on coastal sandstone.

Charley was studying for a BSc, majoring in earth science. Considering she was also an active member of Greenpeace and occasionally joined in protest marches about saving the planet, at some point she wanted to know precisely what she was protesting about on a scientific level.

Indeed, she imagined that one day, instead of carrying a protest sign that read, 'No fossil fuels' or some such, her sign would read something like, 'Xo→Hc+X(t) and T+m/Fout+L+D → GWP of CO_2, CH_4 and N_2O ≥ 500 years:

YOU HAVE BEEN WARNED!' Let's see the politicians ignore that one, she thought.

On this particular day, Charley and her partner were happily zapping sandstone fragments with X-rays, as were the rest of the class at their various workbenches. Eventually, Dr Segway circulated around to Charley and Sue, to see how they were getting on.

"Now you've compensated X-ray emission for silica content, have you?" he asked, looking over his glasses.

"Oh yes," Charley replied, full of enthusiasm. "Goniometer now at nine degrees."

"Silica 87 per cent," Sue offered, rather wearily.

"Good. Excellent."

He began to move on when Charley, in a lowered voice, sidled up to him.

"Dr Segway, what happened to the Black Star? Are we not studying that any more?"

"Ah, well, considering that it appears to be an as-yet-undiscovered element, almost certainly from beyond this solar system – and that it has unusual properties – the Department of Scientific Research have taken it away for further analysis. Also, the Americans have taken a keen interest, apparently."

"Americans? Like, scientists?"

"Yes. They're interested in its atomic properties. That's why it's now over at the research facility. They've got a team sweeping the grounds for more as well, even though we've already done that and found nothing. It's all very top secret. That's why I'm telling you," he said with a wry smile.

"Are we going over to the research centre to study it some more?" Charley asked.

"Not sure. It seems they might be putting in place a secret research programme. With the Americans involved, who knows how undercover it's going to get. I'm just as annoyed about it as you are, but I'll keep pestering them. Hopefully we'll be able to get in there at some point."

Charley guessed this was not good news for IQ. With government security in place, the task of getting the rock now seemed impossible.

After class, Charley headed for the student café to meet George for lunch, as arranged.

George had arrived first and was sitting at a small round table outside in the courtyard, near the begonias. From there, he could see that work was already underway to reinstate the paving where the rock had been dug up. He'd arrived slightly early because he couldn't wait to get out of the house. And of course, finding a park for his scooter was a simple task – you can park the damn things anywhere.

The other reason he was early was because he was trying to find Madison to ask him about the probe droid thingy. George had wandered around the reserve for an hour but couldn't find him, so he came back to the café.

"Hiya," Charley said breezily as she approached.

"Hi," George replied, somewhat more serious.

Charley plonked herself down and leaned forward; a sense of urgency was in the air. George was just opening his mouth to tell her of his early-morning encounter, when she beat him to it.

"There's something weird going on," she said.

"No kidding," George replied, sitting up in surprise.

"Dr Segway said the rock is under security at the research place and American scientists are looking at it."

George raised his eyebrows. "American?"

"Yeah, so we're going to have a hell of a time if IQ really needs it. He does need it, doesn't he?"

"I think so. He won't have the power to break the Earth's gravity without it. That's my understanding anyway."

"Thing is, I doubt our class will get to have a field trip there. It all sounds a bit top secret," Charley said. "I mean, it's not fair. It was our rock – we found it." The rebellious, Greenpeace-protest streak was coming out in her; once Charley got a bee in her bonnet about something, she was pretty determined to charge into battle. "Dr Segway is miffed about it, too. I hope he manages to get us over there. But, I dunno."

George couldn't wait any longer. He had to tell Charley what happened before he burst. He leaned forward. "Hey," he whispered.

"What?" Charley said aloud.

George looked around to make sure no one was within earshot. "I had a *visitor* last night," he murmured, the word visitor accompanied by hand-gestured quotations.

"A *visitor*?" Charley said aloud, imitating George's gestures.

George cringed, quickly glanced around and signalled Charley to talk softly. "Yeah. I was woken up by this thing floating around in the kitchen – some kind of robot thing. Could be what Madison was talking about."

After a slight pause, Charley asked, "What did it do?"

"Nothing much. Just floated around the kitchen, into the lounge, back into the kitchen and disappeared out the back door."

"Floated?"

"Yeah, about a foot off the floor," he explained. "When it went back outside, it disappeared up into the air."

Charley sat back in her chair with a look of suspicion. "Hang on, you've been into the wacky-backy and God knows what else. You've been either hallucinating or dreaming, I'd say."

George hadn't considered this. True, they'd all smoked a joint or two last night, but this was nothing out of the ordinary for George and he had never experienced any hallucinations or any other after-effects from smoking the stuff previously.

He chuckled. "Never thought of that. But a lot of strange things have happened to us recently, don't you think?"

"Oh yes," she whispered, getting anxious. "It's creepy. I mean, who'd believe us, eh?"

"Exactly," George replied. For an instant, they looked closely into each other's eyes. George could feel that magic zing coming on again. He broke off the stare and concentrated on the discussion. "I was trying to find Madison this morning. I wanted to ask him what he thought about us dobbing IQ in to the police or someone. Or maybe Dr Segway could help. What do you think?"

"You can't be serious!" Charley fired back.

George almost reeled. "I just think it's beyond our capabilities to help him. And if he's going to be stuck here, he'll have to come clean eventually. Won't he?"

Charley's demeanour sharpened. "No, you can't think that way. Besides, no one would believe you. They'd think you're mad, like all the other so-called UFO nuts." She lowered her voice to a whisper. "IQ doesn't belong here and we can't let anyone else know. Don't you remember ET?"

George felt like laughing out loud at the thought of IQ as ET, but then quickly suppressed this reaction, partly because Charley seemed so keyed up he thought she might hit him if he did laugh, plus he realised she was probably right. If they worked as a team, and with IQ's superior technology, there must be a way.

"And the other issue is," she continued, "if this stuff gets into the wrong hands ..."

"Mm," George replied. "I think this thing alluded to that. Something about the end of the world."

"That'd be what they'd do, you know," she said. "Why else would the Americans want it?"

"Yeah. We'll talk to IQ later. Give him the latest developments and then try and work out the next move."

"When's that?" Charley asked.

"Well, his ship didn't appear to be in the reserve when I went down there this morning. I'll try again after my acoustics lecture."

"Shall we meet here then? What time does your lecture finish?"

"4.30."

"Fine. God, it's all becoming a bit of a life-or-death situation," she said.

"Well, yeah, I was scared witless by that thing floating around," George complained.

Charley smiled. "Oh, who cares about your floaty thing?" she joked, making them both laugh.

Chapter 16

IQ had been hovering over the scientific research facility, keeping an eye on things – comings and goings, and surveying the inside of the buildings with very clever see-through-things camera technology.

Charley's chip was keeping IQ's ship going and it was getting energy from the sun, but as George quite rightly guessed, it was never going to be enough to get him into space and on his way back to Sirius C. Now that he had a star translayer, or at least something close enough to resembling one, all he wanted was to get home and complete his errand.

In some ways, Earth reminded him of his home planet; the roundness of it, certainly. And the land and the ocean bits were also similar. Sirius C Major was also very green, with lots of jungles, forests, plantations and crops. There weren't any cities as such, or countries. The land was dedicated to all things organic. Revs tended to travel and live on their spaceships. Most industry was carried out underground or within orbiting satellites. Artificial infrastructure on the surface was sparse and generally to do with parking spaceships or collecting solar energy. No one owned land for residential purposes; all living was done on the move, and anyone could freely zip between the three Sirius C planets or beyond.

There were no borders, spaceports or customs. The only authority in terms of running the place and keeping things in order was software based, and this was maintained by the rev population. Anything from changes in the law to the best beaches to visit would be determined by general online consensus, and this in turn kept everything and everyone up to date with all things Sirius.

Compliance was automatic. So, for example, if a speed restriction changed, your spaceship's navcom would update itself and happily oblige. You could never get pulled over for drunk driving, partly because there weren't any police to pull you over, but also because your navcom would know what the law was and it would never allow you to take control of your ship while you were inebriated; your ship knows the traffic laws, so you don't have to – as simple as that.

Although human technology may as well have been in the Stone Age compared to rev technology, life on Earth seemed amazingly overcomplicated to IQ. And the longer he was stranded, the more uneasy he felt. He couldn't see himself adapting to human society. Humans tended to get very emotional, he thought. And human personalities were a lot more diverse than revs'. This made IQ wary of who he could trust.

Getting back to the matter at hand, he asked his navcom about what strategy it recommended for breaking and entering, and stealing the Y2K.

The navcom replied, *Analysis of all access ways, card access codes, electric fence control, infrared detection and video surveillance is complete, and the conclusion is that all the electronic security devices and mechanical locks are easy enough to disable. Piece of cake. The tricky bit will be avoiding being seen, as they are bound to be upset by your presence, particularly the security guards, who, if they are any good, will no doubt be on the lookout for a rock-stealing alien from another planet.*

IQ considered this for a moment, and then asked, *Would a diplomatic approach work? What if we just asked nicely?*

The navcom took a long time to answer and eventually concluded, *Could get messy*.

This confirmed IQ's suspicions; he really needed George and the others as intermediary liaison between him and the rest of the human race.

Let's go back to the reserve, he instructed.

After George's lecture, he met up with Charley and they wandered down to the reserve. As they approached the clearing, they could see IQ's beautiful purple ship sitting on the ground through the trees.

Madison was at the foot of the ramp, waving and grinning maniacally. "After you," he said, bowing slightly and directing them aboard.

"Thank you, sir," Charley said with a smile and a salute.

George was agitated. "Hey, Madison. I got a visit from your probe thingy."

Madison dropped his grin. "Oh dear."

"Come on. I'll tell you all about it inside."

IQ watched the three approach from his monitor screen on the flight deck.

On entering, George was already raving about his probe droid encounter. "This thing floating around my kitchen. Two-thirty in the bloody morning."

"Oh dear," said Madison, genuinely concerned.

They all sat in their usual place on the side couch.

"It was weird, though. It seemed to communicate in some way," he said.

"What did it want?" IQ asked.

"Dunno. I got a bit of a message from it. Well, more of a vibe, really. Some sort of warning." He turned to Madison. "Mean anything?"

Madison slowly nodded his head. "Oh, that," he said, deep in thought.

IQ chipped in, "It would be very unfortunate if Earth's one-and-only piece of Y2K is developed into a weapon of mass destruction. I don't like where this is going."

"No," George replied. "I don't like it either."

"You don't like what?" Charley asked.

"What IQ said," he said.

Charley was perplexed. "But you haven't lit up yet. I thought you had to have a smoke to understand each other?"

There was a brief stunned silence.

"Whatever the probe did to Madison, it has done it to you," IQ said to George.

"Oh dear," Madison said.

George was fumbling for words. "It ... it didn't do anything. Did it? I can't remember."

"What're you talking about?" Charley asked.

"Seems I can now understand IQ-speak."

She looked at him, gobsmacked. "How?"

"Something to do with Madison's probe droid, I suspect. Must have zapped me, too."

"You didn't notice anything at the time?" she asked.

"Well, I was scared out of my wits. I dunno. No after-effects anyway. So do you want to join in on the conversation? If so, I'll have to light up."

"Oh no, don't worry," she said wearily. Then after a pause, "Look, what is this probe thing anyway?"

IQ was sitting in his pilot seat quietly looking at the screen. At last he said, "Seems we have an update." And with a little help from the navcom filling in some of the details, he proceeded to tell the gang all about Star Trackers. George did his best to provide Charley with an abridged version as IQ went along.

Star Trackers were essentially monitor droids owned and operated by the Scorpius-Centaurus Association, from the planet Crux Alumina that orbits the star Acrux – an insignificant star within the Southern Cross constellation. This was a long way away from Earth.

The Scorpius-Centaurus Association, or SCA, was set up centuries ago to promote stability, conservation, preservation, peace, and all-round good vibes in and around the Crux-Centaurus region and beyond. This was deemed necessary following a rough patch when the region wasn't so nice. Planets were suffering from overcrowding, ecologies were going downhill, wars were fought, won, lost, abandoned and then restarted, over trivial things long forgotten about.

The vibes were not good, things were rather nasty, and it was getting to be a bit tiresome for everyone. Then, at some point, a group got together and did some future behavioural modelling in an effort to improve their livelihood. This was eventually achieved by genetic engineering; identifying and promoting the nice genes and zapping out the nasty ones. It was evolution on steroids, and once the programme was rolled out, it became part of their everyday genetic make-up.

The SCA employed Star Trackers to roam the region and keep an eye on things for them. They were not a police force as such, they merely tracked things down for the SCA to consider. Hence the name Star Trackers. The particular model that met Madison was known as a P51

Star Tracker. It was about 3,000 years old – one of the newer models.

Star Trackers were no longer required in the Acrux and Sirius regions because all forms of nasty behaviour had been eradicated. So, with little else to do, they were exploring neighbouring systems.

Although Earth was well outside their monitoring area, this particular Star Tracker was following up on some earlier data about a lump of Y2K landing there millions of years ago. Once Earth was on the radar, some data on evolutionary progress filtered through.

The story goes, things got off to a good start on Earth – the planet was teeming with life and the ecology was perfectly balanced. It all seemed very nice indeed. The best bit was when the inhabitants hadn't discovered fire yet – nor the iPhone, as it turns out. This went on for many millions of years.

Then quite suddenly, one particular species with big ideas began to dominate all the others. Things started going downhill at that point. The ecology was suffering badly, entire species were wiped out, iPhones were invented, and the climate was changing for the worse, creating all sorts of havoc. Clearly, a bit of nastiness was creeping in. It was a waste of a perfectly good habitable zone. Something needed to be done, and the SCA was considering its options.

When IQ finished the story, the group sat silently for a few seconds with sceptical looks on their faces. Except for Madison, of course; he was spooked as usual.

Finally George broke the silence. "Surely the SCA wouldn't approach Earth, would they? I mean, I know we have our problems, but, well, I mean it would be deemed an invasion, wouldn't it?"

IQ glared at him impassively. "They'd do whatever

they felt needed doing without you even knowing."

George hummed cynically. "Hmm ... Quite a story."

IQ then asked, "Would anyone believe you if you told them about meeting me?"

George shrugged. "Probably not. They'd have to meet you, like Steve did, I expect."

"Have you talked to anyone about this Star Tracker?"

"No," George and Madison said together.

"But there are others," Madison said.

"What?" George asked him.

"Others who have been probed by the thing," he said. "Just like me."

"Like who? Well, apart from me," George asked.

"I don't know," Madison said sincerely. "It told me, that's all."

"But of course half the university knows about the rock," George said. "Although, Charley, you still don't know what it is yet, do you?"

"I've learned way more about it here than in class," she said. "It's a bit of a mystery to everyone else."

"And you haven't let on to anyone what we've learned here?"

"No. And luckily no one's mentioned the piece I chipped off. It's weird. I don't think I'd normally do that," she said.

"Do what?"

"Keep it secret. But, I don't know, the stuff draws you in. It's like it has some kind of mesmerising power. It's on our website."

"What website is that?" George asked.

Just then, Charley's geology class's website came up on the screen.

"That's it!" she said. "Hit the blog and see if there've been any updates."

"What?" IQ asked.

Charley stood up and pointed to the forum link on the screen. "Select that."

Without IQ having to move, the forum blog came up and Charley studied the latest entries.

"There!" she exclaimed, pointing at the screen. "From my friend in San Fernando, ah ... 'nuclear science department find it very interesting'. Hmm, I wonder if that's where the American interest came from. Can I reply on that?"

"I expect so," IQ said, a little bored.

"Do you have a keyboard?" she asked.

"Just say what your reply is, the navcom will sort it out," said IQ, slightly impatiently.

Charley was at a bit of a loss. "Sorry, what?"

"Just say what you want to go in there," said George.

"OK ... um, 'Hi Rene, I think your nuclear scientists are here. Unfortunately, our project of studying it has ceased due to government and possibly US scientist involvement.' How about that?"

Charley's reply had been entered just as if she'd typed it out herself.

The four gazed at the screen for a few seconds, each lost in their own thoughts.

At last IQ said, "I think we should keep this to ourselves."

"Right," George replied. Then he translated for Charley.

"Sorry, I can delete it if you want," she offered.

The screen went back to showing what was outside. It was a bird's-eye view of the research centre.

"The Y2K is in there," IQ indicated.

Suddenly, the image showed the inside of the building and they could see staff moving about.

"Right there." He stood up and pointed. "I can disable all security controls. The difficulty is ... all those humans."

“It looks like it’s in a lab,” George said. “There’s test equipment there.” He suddenly flinched as a cacophony of noise filled his head. “Oh, what’s that?”

Madison could hear it, too. “Are we at the zoo?” he asked, looking out the window.

“I’ll see if I can target the area,” IQ said.

George then realised he was hearing what was going on inside the building – people talking, footsteps, doors closing, coffee machines, photocopiers, air conditioning, keyboard tapping. Sounds from all round the building came together as one big horrible noise.

Then the sounds began to change, drift apart, sort themselves out. A graphic came up on the screen as IQ guided the eavesdropping device to the room where the Y2K was. They had to wait a while before they heard anything useful. There was a brief conversation between three men. It seemed the Y2K was destined to be relocated to the States within the next day or two. George explained this to Charley.

“I wonder who those guys are,” he said. It was impossible to see because the view was from directly above.

“Roger Mora, Foreign Liaison Officer, SIS; Professor Dawson, Director of Mineralogy and Geology; and Simon Cooper, Senior Research Technician,” IQ said, matter-of-factly.

“How do you know that?” George asked.

“It’s logged into the security system and encoded on their access control cards,” IQ replied. The screen graphics then added name tags to each of the men.

“Listen,” Charley said. “Why don’t I see Dr Segway when I get back? Now we know Dawson’s involved, we might be able to get a few more clues as to what’s going on.”

“Yes,” agreed George. “Probably better than trying to break in at this point.”

“We need to act fast,” IQ said. He was willing to go along with a cunning plan, but he knew that if all else failed, he could still use force. And that would really make headline news. But then IQ wouldn’t care. He’d be halfway across the solar system before his spaceship was revealed on TV.

“Oh shit!” George exclaimed, suddenly realising what the time was. “I need to get back. We’ve got band practice.”

“OK, we’ll meet up again later and hopefully I’ll have more news,” Charley said.

“When?” George asked.

“I don’t know. I’ll text later tonight.”

They were now back at the reserve. The flight deck door slid silently open and as they got up to go out, George noticed something was missing.

“Hey, where’s Madison?”

“Coming,” Madison called from down the corridor.

“Where did you slink off to?” George asked.

“Oh, just looking around.”

IQ eyed him suspiciously.

The three walked down the ramp and through the bush to the path back to the university.

“Well, best of luck,” George said to Charley. “We’ll catch up later.” He went off to find his scooter.

Charley went to say goodbye to Madison, but he’d already disappeared.

Chapter 17

By the time Steve arrived at George's place, George had his gear all ready for band practice.

"Anything weird going on in here?" Steve asked as he approached the open back door.

"Just the usual," George replied.

"That's a relief. Got your gear all ready?"

"Yep," said George as he hoisted his keyboard case and satchel from the floor. "Let's go."

"I'll take that, if you like," Steve said, reaching for George's keyboard case.

They went out and George locked up behind him.

"How's IQ going with his rock?" Steve asked.

"Well, we know where it is," George replied as he descended the deck steps behind Steve. "At this stage, Charley hopes to get a field trip there with her geology class."

They wandered down the driveway to the street where Steve's car was parked.

"You really like her, don't you?" Steve asked with a grin.

George was suddenly embarrassed and unsure what to say. He was reluctant to give away his true feelings, but yes, he really did like Charley. "Well, maybe," he eventually admitted.

"I like her, too," Steve said. "Yeah, I think she's really bright. She's got a good spirit."

"Yep," George said, looking at the ground in front of him.

They piled into Steve's Subaru station wagon and set off.

"So you've got this song of yours sussed?" Steve asked.

"Yeah," George replied. "I think it will sound fab. I mean, it's pretty easy. And there's plenty of scope to really vamp it out. We can make it as short or as long as we want."

"Sounds cool."

"I only hope Matt is OK with playing along to a sequence."

"Oh, he'll be fine. Nothing fazes Matt the mad drummer."

George laughed. "He'll probably hardly bat an eyelid if he ever met IQ."

"Shit," Steve said under his breath. "Seems like a bit of a dream or something now, but when I was face to face with IQ for the first time, my God, I didn't know what to think."

"I know what you mean. Not really how I would have imagined an alien from out of space to be like."

"How's that?"

"I dunno," George paused to gather his thoughts. "He seems very human in some ways. I guess I would have expected something scarier in an alien. Maybe a bit threatening. You know?"

"Yeah. In some ways he fits the stereotype ..." Steve began.

Suddenly George interrupted, "Oh shit, I forgot to tell you – I can understand IQ without taking any dope!"

"How's that?"

"Well, we think that probe droid thingy did something to me when it entered my house the other night. Like it did to Madison."

"So it entered more than just your house," Steve laughed.

George didn't see the joke.

"OK. That is weird," Steve continued. "So you can hold a conversation with IQ?"

"Yeah."

"Without getting high?"

"Yep."

"Because the actual sound of his speech is just a horrible noise," said Steve. "Do you still hear that? Or is it like when we light up?"

"Oh, it's clear as. It's almost like that thing has uploaded a translation app into my head."

"Who do you think his voice sounds like?" Steve asked.

"Well, kind of sounds like me, really."

"Yeah, same. I mean, like me."

"It's like the voice I hear in my head when I'm reading something. You know?" George said.

"Yeah, exactly."

George gazed out the window for a moment. "I wonder if we're ever going to get over this."

"You mean, how will it end?"

"Yeah. And if other people are going to become involved."

"Well, who knows?"

"Because, this is like one of the biggest things ever, isn't it?" George said.

"Yeah, absolutely."

"I mean, this would be massive news worldwide. Everyone would go nuts if we showed IQ off to the world."

They were quiet for a minute.

Then Steve killed the silence. "Nah! Everyone will think he's a CGI."

Their practice room was in an old office building near the centre of town. It was in a commercial area, so they could make as much noise as they wanted, day or night. A number of rooms in the building were hired out to bands, and when a few of them were practising at the same time, the cacophony anywhere within a 100-metre radius was quite extraordinary. Luckily there was no one around to complain.

Getting into the building was easy; they unlocked the front door. Getting from the lobby to the practice room was the hard bit, especially when they were carrying gear. First off, they would check the lift. And typically this would be out of order. After scaling the grand staircase to the first floor in semi-darkness, they then had to make their way to the windowless side of the building and down a long corridor. Fortunately, the emergency lighting was always on. Unfortunately, the emergency lighting consisted of two dim lights – one at one end of the corridor and one at the other. You took your chances in the middle bit, and that's precisely where the door was for the stairwell. So, after fumbling for the door, it's up two flights of stairs, down two more corridors and, hey presto, Dark City's practice room. Needless to say, the band's name was inspired by this little excursion.

As George and Steve ascended the stairs, the distant thumping of Matt's drums and echoed scream of Razor's guitar came wafting down to meet them.

When Steve opened the practice room door, the sledgehammer sound wave almost stopped them in their tracks. If Steve had been playing as well, it certainly would have stopped them.

Once in, George and Steve began setting up their gear while being mercilessly pounded by Matt and Razor crashing and banging away.

It's funny, George thought, if you're playing along, the noise is no problem. But if you're trying to do something else that requires a reasonable amount of concentration, it's like something out of boot camp with this infernal racket blasting at you. No wonder roadies lose so many brain cells. Although noise level is probably the least of their worries.

At last George was set up and plugged into the PA. He selected the 'Black Star' sequence, turned the level up and pushed the go button. The sound was electric. Matt quickly changed his beat to play along with the sequence. Razor glanced over and recognised the chord of the opening riff George was playing, and boom, he was in. Steve sauntered over with his bass round his knees, glanced at George's handwritten notes and quickly began thundering away and nodding his head like fury. The song took off.

At last, after ten minutes of heinous thrashing, they ground to a halt, smiling and congratulating each other on a job well done.

Matt piped up from behind the drum set. "What *is* that?"

"New song," said George, keeping explanations to a minimum while Steve was still filling the airspace by working through his basslines.

"It's cool," Matt replied, and emphasised the point with a crashing drum roll.

"Got any words?" Razor asked, while cracking open another beer.

"Yep."

Just as Steve came over to have a look through George's lyrics, Matt started up again. George had previously learned that quick thinking was the key when introducing new material during practice, because at least one of the four was always banging away while others were trying to suss something out.

Steve had a quick read and gave the thumbs-up sign. “Let’s go for another one,” he yelled, and positioned the lyric sheet where he could see it.

As they were going for another take, George saw his phone light up with a text. Once they’d finished, he checked the message. It was from Charley: *Seems we have more time. Rock going to US Wednesday 12th.*

George texted back: *U sure?*

Yep. Had meeting with segway and dawson. We visit rock soon. More tomorrow.

Wednesday the 12th; that was four days after the Summer Sizzler. George wasn’t sure how much to believe about the whole SIS and American thing. And he always eyed anyone in a suit with suspicion.

“Let’s go over the rest of the set,” Steve suggested.

George put his phone down and selected another sound on his synth. The band played through a short set of their best numbers in preparation for the Sizzler gig. Even though George wasn’t going to play these songs at the gig, he joined in at a reduced level for the remainder of practice.

He wasn’t concentrating too much on the music; his head was full of questions. He was thinking of a way to see Charley after practice without alerting Steve about it. He still felt uneasy about anyone knowing about his affection for her.

“Now, you’re not playing these on the day, are you?” Matt asked George when they’d finished.

“Only ‘Getting There’ and that new one,” George replied.

"Good," Matt said with a nod.

"I'm sorry if I cramp your style," George joked sarcastically. "Maybe I'll just play maracas."

"No, don't do that," Razor laughed.

Matt elaborated. "No, I meant good in that we're doing the new one. It's a killer," he said and proceeded to lay into his drum kit like his life depended on it.

George yelled at Steve. "We doing any more?"

"If you want. We'll have another run-through tomorrow night."

"I'm OK for now. When do you want to head off?"

"Yeah, we can go," Steve said as he hoisted his bass off his shoulder.

The session over, George and Steve waved goodbye as they headed out the door. They left Matt and Razor shredding some speed metal, their din slowly receding as George and Steve made their way back downstairs.

George figured he'd probably have time to jump on his scooter and shoot round to Charley's place once Steve dropped him off. But when he got home, he changed his mind. Maybe it wasn't that urgent for now.

He plopped down on the couch, noticing an empty space where the TV had been, and thought about what IQ was doing. It seemed so surreal. Somewhere in the city was a being from another planet that only the four of them knew about. Maybe IQ's ship was above him now, he thought. Watching his every move. Maybe not. Not really IQ's style. Besides, IQ wouldn't want to waste any power.

He dug his phone out of his satchel and texted Charley: *Wot time tomorrow?*

There was no immediate reply.

Interestingly, there was no talk of IQ on the way home with Steve. Discussion was more about the Summer

Sizzler. It was a big gig for the band. It would hopefully promote them to a wider range of events. The gig would be recorded, and the plan was to use that set as the basis for their first album. As Steve had so optimistically pointed out, 'What could possibly go wrong?'

George leaned his head on the back of the couch and closed his eyes. What would happen if they all forgot about IQ? he thought. Just left him to sort himself out. Would he have to phone home?

If IQ could get here, so could his mates. They could come in mighty star-destroyer ships threatening Earth with their dry wit and sarcasm. And when communication links were sorted out, they'd say it was all George's fault; he didn't help their friend IQ.

George woke with a start. It was very dark and he was sure he'd left the kitchen light on.

Oh no, not again, he thought.

He slowly raised his head from the back of the couch. His neck was stiff and sore. He leaned forward and scanned as much as the room as he could without moving too much. There was nothing obvious, but he had an uneasy feeling. He gingerly lowered himself to the floor and turned around. From his crouching position, over the back of the couch, he could see the kitchen. Who was he kidding? It was dark; he couldn't see a bloody thing. Just then, movement caught his eye. He stared at the darkened shape. It had moved, he was sure of it.

His legs began to go all pins and needles. Oh great, he thought. Just when I need to run like hell, my legs won't work.

Movement again. Yes, he could make out a shape. A familiar shape. The droid was back.

This time, George felt he ought to glean a bit more information from the thing. He wanted to make contact. "I can see you, you know," he said at the darkened kitchen. "What do you want?"

The Star Tracker floated past the dining table and came over towards the couch. George bravely stood his ground, or rather, squatted. It began to move around the couch.

He had to adjust his defensive position. He had to stand up. However, because all his attention centred on the Star Tracker, he forgot about his pins and needles. He tried to stand, but only managed to fall backwards. He desperately reached out to the edge of the coffee table to try and hoist himself up. It didn't go well. He stumbled backwards, caught a foot on the table leg, fell on the carpet bum first, and did a backwards roll to finally come to rest sitting on the floor with his back against the wall.

He sat there in the vacant space where his TV had been. His mind raced through a roundabout process of deduction. IQ took the TV. He needs it for something or other – George never really understood that bit, but he needed it nonetheless. IQ also needed the Y2K rock to power his spaceship. Since IQ came on the scene, this droid thing, which had been bothering Madison all these years, suddenly turned its attention to George. What was the deal?

"Are you after the Y2K rock?" he asked it. Then bravely added, "You can't have it. We're getting it for IQ."

The Star Tracker answered, but not in anything vaguely resembling English. It was more a vibe that came over George, a calming sensation. He seemed to get the message that everything would be all right, followed by the same sort of warning-of-doom it had given him the night before.

It then floated away, through the kitchen and out the back door. The kitchen light came on again.

George knew what he had to do. He had to help IQ get his Y2K. He couldn't let it fall into the hands of the human race. The human race depended on it. He had to call someone.

He struggled to his feet and grabbed his phone from the couch. Its display showed 12.37 am. Maybe too late to call Charley. He'd see her first thing in the morning, that's what he'd do. Straight after breakfast. Once he got to uni. After his programming lab. Yes, that's it. He'd definitely see her sometime tomorrow. Hopefully.

There was a text. George almost reeled; it was from Charley: *C u tomorrow 10 am.*

Yes, that would do nicely, he thought.

He went over to the back door and peered out at the darkness. All was still and quiet. He closed the door and activated his burglar alarm. He then went over and plonked himself down on the couch and gazed at the vacant space where his TV had been.

Chapter 18

The next morning, George rode his scooter to uni with great purpose. He was on a mission. He had to see Charley. He also wanted to catch up with Madison. Indeed, he had a feeling that Madison knew more about the Star Tracker droids than he was letting on. He wanted to know if they were anything to worry about. Or, specifically, anything for IQ to worry about.

It's funny, he thought, Madison seemed to be the missing link in all this. He came on the scene almost by chance, yet was fast becoming an indispensable part of the team. They just had to prise out of him the information they needed.

George parked his scooter in his usual spot in the car park – an unspecified gap between the driveway and the fence. He didn't have a parking permit, but they never seemed bothered with rogue scooters. Luckily there was another scooter parked there and he followed the tradition and pulled up alongside and planted the stand. He was happy to see that his scooter had more mirrors.

He was on his way to the computer lab in the main block when his thoughts eventually led him to the inevitable getting-out-the-phone. He stood in the middle of the foyer and began texting Charley. Students were passing by in all directions.

"Hello, handsome."

George jumped and whirled to his left to see Charley beaming at him.

"Oh, I was just texting you," he said.

"Well," Charley said with pizzazz, "here I am!"

"Indeed ..." George replied, a bit lost for words.

They stood staring at each other for a few seconds. Charley added a flourish to her expression as a cue to move George along.

Which he finally did. "I just wondered what you were up to this morning," he said, pocketing his phone.

"I'm going to see Dr Segway. He's trying to make a time for us at the research facility."

"Right. When are you going to do that?"

"Now," she said. "Wanna come?"

"Yeah, sure. I'll tag along. Where're we going?"

"Earth Science block. Come on."

She grabbed him by the hand and they set off out the other side of the foyer, Charley leading the way, George floating along like a great gangly balloon. Holding Charley's hand, he truly felt like he was walking on air.

Charley knocked on Dr Segway's office door. She was still holding on to George's hand, which he was beginning to get a little nervous about. How professional would it look negotiating with the powers that be while they were holding hands? Might be useful if some of the party were dead and they were having a seance. Maybe he could pretend to be blind, George thought, with Charley as his guide person to guide him around the place. No that wouldn't work, Charley would have to be in on it. Maybe he should say he has to go to class, and run away. Maybe he could feign a panic attack.

Suddenly the door handle rattled and turned. The sound shattered George's inane daydreams and he snapped back to reality. The door opened and to George's relief, Charley let go of his hand.

"Hi, Dr Segway," she said.

"Oh, hello, Charlene. Come on in."

They shuffled into his windowless office. The room was quite small, just enough space for a desk, chair and a couple of filing cabinets. The shelves were cluttered with all sorts of geological paraphernalia.

"This is my friend George," she said. "He's studying sound engineering."

"Oh, I'm sorry," Dr Segway joked. "So you'll know all about the acoustic properties of the refurbished foyer."

"Oh, ah ..." George said vaguely. His eyes settled on a Rubik Cube up on the shelf above Dr Segway's desk.

"Just having you on," Segway said. "It has none." He turned to Charley. "Charlene, we have an answer. Wednesday the fifth."

"For a field visit?"

"Yes."

"Oh great." Charley beamed at George.

George was meaning to respond positively and say something like 'yeah', but it came out, "Ugh."

Dr Segway continued, "We'll use our geology lecture period for it. I'll be sending out an email later today."

"Great," said Charley. "Is it still going to the States?"

"Looks that way. I'll be catching up with Professor Dawson later. He has a visitor coming from San Fernando."

"San Fernando?" Charley said, somewhat surprised. "San Fernando University? In California?"

"Yes, that's right. A nuclear scientist as I understand it."

Charley's head was reeling. What were the chances

of this scientist coming from the same place as her good friend and study correspondent?

Segway continued, "Anyway, looks like we're losing it."

"Pity."

"Yes. Very frustrating," Dr Segway said, showing his annoyance. "Amazing discovery. Nothing else like it on the planet. It would tell us a lot about distant worlds. Makes moon rocks seem trivial."

He reached up to a shelf and took down a small black rock, about the size of a walnut.

"Here, have a look at this," he said and gave it to George to look at.

George turned it over in his fingers. "What is it?"

"It's a moon rock. Ilmenite basalt. Dead boring."

He took the rock off George and put it back up on the shelf. George was stunned. He couldn't believe he just touched a moon rock. Charley had already seen it; she wasn't particularly fussed about seeing it again. George, on the other hand, was mesmerised by the little black rock. He stared at it up on the shelf. He desperately wanted another look.

"Well, what's the legal standing on this?" Charley asked. "Doesn't it belong to the university?"

"It did until the government stepped in," Segway explained. "Nothing we can do, I'm afraid. Anyway, watch out for the email."

"Yep, sure. Thanks, Dr Segway. Come on, George."

George was making a feeble attempt to indicate that he wanted to fondle the moon rock again, but Charley led him out.

"That sounds promising, doesn't it?" she said as they walked down the corridor.

"Wow, that was incredible!" said George, seemingly star-struck. "Amazing!"

"Er, yeah ..." said Charley, rather perplexed by George's gooey behaviour.

"Oh man, a rock from the moon," he enthused. "I actually touched a rock from the moon. Can we go back in there sometime?"

Charley laughed. "If you're a good boy."

Madison spent the morning ferreting through his collection of stuff in his hospital hidey-hole. Today he felt in the mood for a bit of reorganisation. He needed to sort things out, get things done, make plans. It was a busy life being homeless. Or could be, if you were totally obsessed with other people's rubbish, because there was certainly plenty of it about.

In no particular order, he fussed about the place, moved stuff around and mumbled to himself. Occasionally he would marvel at an item in his collection and shake his head in disbelief that people would actually throw such things away.

He found a garden rake behind a stack of street signs, leaning against the wall. This wasn't right, he thought, rakes should be in the gardening zone, over by the window. He picked it up. He'd forgotten about the rake. It was a good find at the time, and he was very pleased to know he still had it. He was at the point of getting all emotional about how the handle was attached to the head when a familiar sensation came over him.

He suddenly looked up, his eyes darting madly around the room. He held up the rake in a defensive pose and gingerly made his way over to the one-and-only window and peered out. It didn't take long to confirm his suspicions. Outside, amongst a stack of old stainless-steel sanitisers, was the Star Tracker. Or 'probe droid' as Madison called it.

He stared at it, wide-eyed. He knew what was coming; he was about to get an update on all things probe. When he first met it, a few years ago, it basically interrogated him. That's what it felt like anyway. Although it didn't actually speak, Madison could tell what it wanted. It was as if it sucked the information out of his brain.

What Madison didn't know was that it also did this to a number of other people on the same frequent basis. And this was just as well; it would be a sad outlook if an extraterrestrial impression of humans was based on Madison as a shining example. Further visits were much less severe, fortunately. It still gave him the jitters, though.

"A bit early, aren't you?" he asked it. He was sure it hadn't been that long since its last visit.

The reply felt like something to do with urgent business. Something was going down, something was being planned, and it seemed Madison was about to become part of whatever it was up to whether he liked it or not. Once again he got the vibe of impending doom.

"Are there more of you here?" he asked as he held up the rake in a 'don't mess with me' pose.

A knock at the door made him jump. He whirled around and pointed the rake at the door.

"Madison," a familiar voice yelled. "Are you in there? It's George."

Madison scampered over to the door, being careful not to trip on anything. With his rake at the ready, he flung open the door and was greeted by George.

George held his hands up. "I surrender," he said. Then asked, "You all right?"

Madison peered outside, eyes darting left and right. "Quick. Come in."

"What's up?" George asked as he entered.

Madison did another quick scan outside then quickly shut the door and braced the rake up against it. He turned to George and put his finger to his lips, then motioned for George to follow. He went over to the window and pointed, gesturing at George to look.

George peered out the window. "What am I supposed to be seeing here, Madison?" he asked quietly.

Madison looked out. "It's gone!"

"What's gone?"

"The probe. It was there, I tell you. It was out there," he said, pointing to the spot.

"Well I got another visit last night. Unless it was a dream," George said vaguely.

"No!" Madison insisted, grabbing George's arm and making him jump again. "No, it isn't. No. It's real. Oh yes."

George could see Madison was obviously worked up, so he deliberately tried to calm things down. "Well, whatever. We're forming a plan of attack to get the Y2K for IQ."

"What?" Madison exclaimed, as if it was all new to him.

"Charley has a field trip to the research place on Wednesday, and we're going to do the deed. Get the rock. So to speak."

"Oh my!" Madison said. He looked worried.

"Don't worry, we won't telesend you again. Between IQ's surveillance technology and Charley acting as the insider, we'll pull the biggest job in history."

"Yes," Madison said, nodding thoughtfully. "So what do you want me to do?"

"Well, you're part of the team," George said as he made his way back to the door. "Jeez, what is all this crap?" he asked, indicating at Madison's treasure lying around the place.

"Just doing a bit of spring cleaning," Madison replied modestly.

"OK," George said doubtfully. "So you're allowed to live here?"

"Oh yes," Madison said. "Well, possibly." Then added, "No one's objected."

"Probably because no one knows you're here."

"Who doesn't know?" Madison asked, looking spooked again.

George shrugged. "Anyone."

"Oh," said Madison, relieved. "But I do look after the place. You just caught me on a bad day, that's all. I'm doing some tidying. See?" he said, gesturing reassuringly at his messy hovel.

"Right." George looked around briefly. "How long have you been here?"

"Oh, a few years, I think," Madison said vaguely. "Yes, a few years."

"Where were you before that?"

"Oh, around," he said even more vaguely. "Around."

"So this would have been a good find then," George said as he removed the rake and opened the door.

"Yes. Yes indeed. I have lots of room to put my things," he said with pride. "Everything's changed now, though. I have to get things ready."

"Yeah, right," said George, not really listening. "But where did you live before you were, um, homeless?"

"Oh, I'm not homeless," Madison insisted.

"Well, you know, before you had, like, an unofficial address, shall we say."

"I do have an official address," Madison said, somewhat baffled at George's line of questioning.

"Do you?"

"Yes."

"What, here?" George asked.

"No. I have a house up in Browns Bay," Madison replied.

"You own a house?" George was somewhat sceptical.

"Yes," Madison said with wide-eyed sincerity.

"So why do you live here? Why not stay in your house?"

Madison looked around, drew close to George and whispered, "Someone else is in there."

George replied quietly, "Who?"

Madison thought for a second. "Brian!" he blurted out, making George jump again.

"Who's he?"

"My tenant," Madison replied, as if it were obvious.

George smiled and shook his head, finally relieved that that little mystery was cleared up. Or maybe half cleared up. There was obviously more to Madison than met the eye. But George figured they'd get to know each other soon enough.

"OK. That's great, Madison. Good for you."

"Yes," Madison continued. "I was just talking to him the other day in the pub," he reminisced, as if it had anything to do with anything. He leaned closer to George and whispered, "Did you know ..." he looked around to make sure no one was within earshot, "... he has a dog."

George pretended to understand completely. "That's great, Madison. All right, we'll be in touch, OK?"

Madison almost stood at attention. "Righto!"

Chapter 19

On the morning of the Summer Sizzler gig, George and Steve had arrived early to carry out their various setting-up activities. George was working with the sound guys to put together a slave PA set-up to demo SoundLive to some music industry reps. Although SoundLive was not going to be controlling the main PA directly, he was confident his demonstration would be good enough. His other duties for the day were stage monitor mixer assistant and playing keyboards for three Dark City numbers.

The gig was held at a local sports stadium. Various local, national and international bands and acts were scheduled to perform during the course of the day. There were two stages set up, the main one on the playing field and a smaller one on a large grass area at the back of the main stand. Around the perimeter of the field stood various caravans, tents and kiosks selling the usual array of refreshments, accessories and souvenirs. The largest tent housed the Sizzler café where the band planned to meet an hour before the event started.

Steve's band was on in the first set, so he was making sure their backline equipment was stacked in the appropriate order backstage and that the stage manager and stagehands knew what they were doing. He really wanted to talk to the stage manager, but he was nowhere to be seen. Instead, he had to explain the band's requirements to a couple of stagehands. When it came to dealing with them, Steve knew it was a real hit-or-miss affair.

Stagehands get their jobs one of two ways: either they're musicians themselves, or they're mates of musicians and have just lucked into the job. With these fellows, Steve was thinking the latter. Once a stagehand gets a backstage pass around their necks, he thought, they think they know everything.

"Now, you got that? That's my bass amp and quad – that'll be behind me, centre. Right? We usually mike the lower-right speaker. Right? And of course, I'll have a vocal mike on a boom. That's Razor's guitar stack and it will be to the left of mine. Right? Mike the lower left of Razor's quad. He's got a vocal mike too. Also, you got ..."

"You want two mikes on the guitar stack?" said Stagehand 1, looking up from his iPad.

"No. Just one usually, lower left. Right?" said Steve.

"And one on the stack," said Stagehand 2.

"The stack?" Steve queried.

"Yes, mike the stack," said Stagehand 2.

"Mike who?" Stagehand 1 asked.

Steve ignored him. "Well, mike the speaker in the stack. Lower left, OK? On Razor's quad."

"Oh!" Stagehand 2 finally realised. "You mean mike the quad."

"Yeah," said Steve. He was beginning to think he was in a Dr Seuss story. "Mike the quad, lower left. Mine's lower right. Right?"

"Right," said Stagehand 1, and selected something on his iPad.

"And George's keyboard stack left of the drums. Right?"

"OK, so that's just in front of the horn section," said Stagehand 1.

"We don't have a horn section," Steve replied.

"Ah, well that's what it says here," said Stagehand 1. "Look," he said, showing Steve the diagram.

"That's for The Palisades," said Steve, pointing to the band name at the top of the screen. "We're Dark City, fourth in the order."

"Dark City?" Stagehand 1 said as he flicked over a few screens. "No, you're, ah, you come on just after Streaky 3, so you're number four."

"That's what I said, we're fourth on," said Steve. He grabbed the iPad. "Let's have a look." He studied the diagram for a few seconds. "Yep, that looks right." He handed it back. "Dark City; there you go," he said, tapping the stencilled band label on the side of his quad. "It's all here."

The stage iPads were Wi-Fi linked, so Scotty, the mix engineer, could see the changes being made on his. "Christ almighty," he said. "Wa are thes bawsaws plain ah?"

"Not a problem," said Stagehand 1 to Steve. "Leave it to us. No problemo."

Steve left them to it and, shaking his head, went off to find George.

Fortunately when Dark City played later in the day, the set-up was indeed correct.

Not so lucky for The Pallisades, however. They were greeted with four mikes on the guitarist's single speaker combo amp, no horn section mikes, the bass amp on the wrong side of the stage and the drum riser behind the back curtain. But this didn't deter them, as they launched into their first number with an extended drum solo intro from an unseen drummer while the stage crew scampered around the stage putting things right, all the while thinking that if they bend over slightly, the audience won't see them.

Meanwhile, George was in the process of testing the channels on the stage monitor mixer when Steve approached.

"Yo, bro. You all set?" Steve asked.

"Hi," said George. "Yeah, no problem. Gear OK?"

Steve laughed. "Who knows with those fellas." He gestured backstage. "Razor and Matt headed for the oxygen tent."

"Oh that'll help."

"I said we'd all meet up at the café."

"Coffee break then?" George suggested.

"Yeah, sure."

"I'll just check where Charley is," George said as he dug his phone out and dialled. "Hi. Yeah. Steve and I are heading over to the café ... far end of the field. OK, cool." He hung up. "She's at the main gate, so we'll meet her over there."

The two made their way backstage, down to ground level and back around to the right side of the structure where all the power equipment, standby generator and recording and broadcast mobiles were situated. The area was screened off on all sides with access ways at the front and back for authorised pass-holders. Stagehands, technicians and riggers were busy moving in and out of the area looking as if they had important things to do.

As George and Steve passed through, George suddenly stopped. "Oh shit!" he said with a look of utter surprise.

"What?" Steve asked.

"What the heck?" George exclaimed. He was staring at something over between the container-enclosed standby generator and the broadcast truck.

"What?" Steve said, frantically looking around.

George pointed as he half-whispered, "That probe thing. It's there!"

"Huh? What're you talking about?" Steve peered in the direction George was pointing and took a few tentative steps towards the broadcast truck. Suddenly he stopped. He could see it. Somehow the thing seemed to blend in to the equipment surrounding it. "What is it?" he hissed back to George.

"I don't know exactly. Actually, I don't know at all. Some kind of space probe, I think," he said in a lowered voice. "Madison first mentioned it, and then it broke into my flat the other night. And last night. I wonder if it's the same one or if there are more of them."

"Madison?" Steve questioned.

Suddenly George was agitated. "Shit, this could be it!"

"This could be what?"

"The thing said something about an invasion," said George. Then vaguely added, "I think."

"An invasion?" Steve replied. "Those guys?"

"Yeah. Well, not so much an invasion. More like a massive probe. Oh I don't know. It's hard to explain. No wonder Madison found it hard to talk about. The thing doesn't speak to you, you get a vibe."

"A vibe?" asked Steve.

"Yeah."

"OK. Let's go vibe," Steve said bravely as he started approaching the Star Tracker.

"Hang on," said George. "Follow me."

He sneaked over to the far left of the barricaded area and around the back of the huge generator container, which, being a standby generator, was dutifully standing by and therefore, thankfully, silent. It was parked at the foot of a grass bank, so George and Steve were relatively concealed as they crept to the other end of the container and peered round the corner. The Star Tracker droid was still there.

George started the communication in his usual style. "Ah ..."

The droid remained motionless.

George tried again. "Ah, what are you doing here?" he asked it.

Still no response.

"I'm getting no vibes, Steve," he hissed over his shoulder.

"Nor am I," Steve said from behind.

George slowly reached out and waved at the Star Tracker's eye. "Hello."

Still nothing.

He stared at the droid for a few seconds, waiting for it to do something.

"What's happening there?" Steve asked.

Suddenly George's phone rang. "Oh, Christ!" he yelled as he stumbled back around the corner, falling over Steve, and the pair of them ended up sprawled on the ground.

Steve looked up and saw the droid floating into view around the end of the container. "Holy shit!" he cried.

"Hello?" he heard George say calmly.

George was on his phone. "Ah, can I get back to you?" he said. "Something's come up. OK, bye."

He hung up and scrambled to his feet. "Now listen," he said assertively. "Now, I don't know what you want or what you're doing, but, ah, well ..."

He pointed a finger at the droid. It seemed to have an effect. The droid backed off around the end of the container, out of sight of George and Steve.

George bravely followed it. "Oh!" he cried, as he stared stupidly at the space where the Star Tracker had been.

"Wha- … what's happening?" Steve said as he got to his feet.

"It's gone," said George, from around the corner. Steve joined him.

"The freakin' thing's gone," George said, somewhat flabbergasted.

"Gone where?"

"I dunno. It just disappeared. It's not fair!"

"Why's that?"

"Well, the frigging thing keeps turning up and I don't know why. It's like it's following me around. I thought maybe it was … I dunno … hostile or something."

Steve moved past George in order to assess the situation for himself. There was nothing more to report. It all seemed quiet and relatively probe free.

Suddenly George jumped wildly as his phone rang again. He shot an exasperated look at Steve and rolled his eyes. "Christ!" he murmured as he answered it. "Hi. Ah, sorry about that. We found one of those probe things, but it's gone now. Oh … tell you later. Yeah, OK." He hung up. "That was Charley. Shall we go?"

"Yeah. Let's go and talk to some humans."

Meanwhile, a meeting was in place at the Department of Scientific Research complex. Topic of discussion was the fate of the Y2K rock. In attendance were John Davies, San Fernando University Director, Professor Hal Dawson, Auckland University Director, Agent Roger Mora, Security Intelligence Service, and Simon Cooper, Research Technician.

Of course, the team didn't call the Y2K by its proper name, because they didn't know about its origin. They also didn't call it by the name the students had given it –

Black Star. Their provisional name for it was 'Project X'.

"When's the earliest we can ship?" Davies asked.

"Give us four hours and we can get it on the next available flight," Mora replied.

"I would be uneasy shipping it depressurised," Davies said. "Are we able to use military transport with a pressurised cargo hold?"

The other three looked at each other with doubtful expressions.

Roger Mora grimaced. "Ooh, the military," he said painfully while wiping his brow.

"Problem?" Davies asked. "I can get a US transporter, if need be," he suggested. "A C17 maybe. It'll take a couple of days to get here. But if you guys have something suitable, we should go."

"I believe our air force has a plane," Mora sighed. "I'll find out if it's working."

The joke went right over Davies' head. "Great," he said, beaming.

"Have we got a contact at the other end?" Mora asked.

"Yep. Top Dog, Los Alamos Lab."

Hal Dawson laughed. "Top Dog? Do we have a name?"

"No. That's all you need to know," Davies said. "Trust me. Address it to Top Dog. It'll get there."

"What about government representation during transit?" Mora asked. "I mean, I can escort it to 'Top Dog', but you might want your own ... security," he said, complete with hand-gestured inverted commas.

"I believe we have FBI agents on the way here now. You're welcome to join them during transit. Up to you."

"I'll come," Mora insisted.

"Sure," Davies replied. He turned to research technician Simon Cooper. "And Simon, you'll accompany me to Los Alamos as well. That right?"

"That's correct. I'm anxious to meet 'Top Dog'," he said with a laugh. "Sorry, no, I'm anxious to set up a data-sharing process."

Once again the joke went right over John Davies' head. "Right."

"Well that sounds easy," Dawson said. "We'll reconvene when your agents arrive."

About the same time, a duo of US Government agents touched down at Auckland International Airport after a 12-hour flight from Houston. Entering the arrival hall, the pair, a man and a woman in their late thirties, approached the driver displaying their name card.

"Reiner and Foley, that's us," the man said.

The man was FBI agent, Will Reiner. He was slim build, slightly taller than average, remarkably clean-shaven after a 12-hour flight, with very neat, short dark hair. Agent Dianne Foley was also slight, but shorter than Agent Reiner, with shoulder-length red hair. They were both casually dressed for the flight.

"Welcome to New Zealand, Mr Reiner, Ms Foley. You all set to go to the Scientific Research Centre?" the driver asked.

"We'll check in to the airport hotel to change, first. And we'll hire a car, so we won't need your services just yet," Reiner replied.

"As you wish. I'll take you over to the hotel," the driver said. "And you can hire a car there."

As they were walking to the exit, the driver turned to Reiner. "By the way, we drive on the left here. You OK with that?"

Reiner and Foley exchanged puzzled looks.

"Tell you what," Reiner said to the driver, "how about

you drive us? If you could give us a few minutes at the hotel. And then we'll go to the centre after that."

"Sure, no problem. Right this way."

Half an hour later, dressed in business attire, the pair were on their way to the Scientific Research Centre.

Reiner got his phone out. "I'm just gonna call John Davies."

"John, Agent Will Reiner, FBI. How's it going? ... yep, just got here ... ah-huh ... right, we're on our way. See you there."

He put his phone away. "John's gonna meet us there."

"He's got it all in hand?" Foley asked.

"Sounds like it."

"I still fail to see why we need to be here at all, Reiner."

"Just to supervise security, Foley."

"Security for a lump of quartz?"

"A lump of quartz with very special qualities, Foley. It has multiple piezo-like resonances and unusual isotope behaviours. The thing vibrated itself out of the ground. Did you know that?"

"I understand all that, Reiner. I've read the file. I just don't see why it has to be a case."

"Give it time, Foley. This is an unknown element we're dealing with." He paused for a few seconds, then leant towards her. "You know it's from outer space."

The driver's eyes glanced at them through the rear-view mirror.

Foley shrugged. "Possibly. Meteorites hit Earth all the time, but what's that got to do with anything?"

Reiner turned to gaze out the car window. "Well," he said thoughtfully, "the truth is out there, Foley. The truth is out there."

Chapter 20

Later that morning, while George, Steve and Charley were at the Summer Sizzler, IQ thought he'd spend some time hovering over the Scientific Research Centre, keeping an eye on comings and goings, and generally sussing things out.

However, just as he arrived on the scene, his navcom alerted him that they weren't the only ones sussing things out – the Star Tracker was there. It had apparently arrived earlier and was currently talking to a heat exchanger. The monitor screen zoomed in on a storage area out in the rear compound of the complex. There, amongst the storage containers and various bits of machinery, the Star Tracker was sitting, or floating, as Star Trackers tend to do.

The navcom picked up the odd signal emitted from the Star Tracker, but nothing of interest. There also appeared to be a power system alarm active in the building. The navcom couldn't figure out why, as the power seemed fine.

Has the Star Tracker detected us? asked IQ.

Affirmative, came the reply.

It all seemed a bit suspicious to IQ. It was quite shrewd

that the Star Tracker should interrogate a heat exchanger, because everybody knows heat exchangers never lie. IQ was also puzzled as to why the Star Tracker was following them around. What the heck was it up to?

Maybe Madison might shed some light, he thought. Madison may come across as being not completely all there, but he knew more than he let on. It was just a matter of asking him the right questions so he didn't get freaked out. There was more to that old human than met the eye, IQ was sure of it. The rest of the gang were at the Summer Sizzler, so maybe it would be a good time to interrogate Madison a bit.

The navcom suddenly interrupted his train of thought with the navcom version of the phrase 'speak of the devil'. The monitor screen panned across to the street. A lone, pathetic-looking figure, who went by the name of Madison, was slowly shuffling along the footpath outside the complex boundary fence.

In that instant, the navcom started receiving a flurry of complex signals from the Star Tracker. It appeared to be waiting for Madison. Something was going down.

Just then, an electricity service vehicle turned off the street into the main gate. It paused at the security gatehouse for a few seconds, the barrier arm lifted and the vehicle went on through. It made its way over to the incoming substation at the front of the building, where it came to a stop. The guard left the gatehouse and walked over to the substation. The electrical technician got out of the vehicle and the two had a brief chat about what the problem was. The guard then unlocked the substation door and the two of them entered.

Without adjusting his ambling, shuffling pace, Madison made his way through the main gate, brazenly skirted the barrier arm, ignored the gatehouse and headed towards the main building. When he was about halfway across the car park, he stopped, looked up at IQ's ship, grinned like an idiot and waved manically. He was holding something up with his other hand. IQ's monitor screen zoomed in; it was the telesender. It was back in the form of George's TV remote.

Madison then overemphasised mouthing of the words, 'I've got the telesender' while pointing to the telesender with his other hand, then made a thumbs-up sign, grinned a bit more and nodded spastically. Once he'd completed his demented series of signals, he slowly continued towards the main entrance of the complex.

IQ couldn't quite believe it. Surely this wasn't in the plan. Was Madison about to blow the whole mission?

Just then the navcom piped up. *The Star Tracker has just disabled the security cameras and access control system.*

This was all completely unexpected. Was the Star Tracker helping Madison steal the Y2K? IQ wondered. They seemed to be one step ahead.

Madison was on a mission. He hadn't really thought about how he was going to fulfil it; that level of detail was not all that important. He had a hunch, a gut feeling, a driving ambition. And these things took priority over a prepared plan of execution any day. Logic and rationale can be things for others to worry about. As George put it, he was part of the team, and he was doing his bit.

He was just a few steps from the main door, when he heard a clattering sound towards the right corner of the building: a large motor-driven roller door was opening. Never one to miss an opportunity, he changed his course and headed for that.

Meanwhile, in the security monitoring room, the security officer had been watching Madison's approach to the main entrance on the video surveillance monitors when suddenly everything went blank. He called the gatehouse, but the security guard was distracted with the electrical technician at the substation.

Madison made it to the roller door and peered around the edge of the opening. It was access into a large workshop area, and there didn't appear to be anybody about. Fortunately, right in the centre of the floor, was the Y2K rock, sitting on a trolley with various bits of test equipment positioned around it.

Madison's face brightened with excitement and determination, and he slipped inside and headed straight for the rock, completely oblivious to security cameras, and totally unconcerned if anyone was in the vicinity.

If there was one thing Madison had learned over the years, it was acting all naïve and innocent will get you out of most tricky situations. This was usually fairly easily achievable, considering he already looked like a harmless idiot at the best of times.

This time, however, there was no one around, and he wandered over to the rock and placed the telesender on it. There, he thought, as he lightly clapped his hands together and prided himself on a job well done.

The rock was nothing like Madison had ever seen. Its black surface seemed as shiny as a mirror, yet as deep as space itself. The material was slightly translucent, and he had the feeling he was looking deep into the heart of the thing, like looking into the universe. He ran his hand over the smooth, shiny surface. For an instant, he was mesmerised by some unseen energy. He suddenly snapped out of it when one of the nearby test machines went 'beep'.

He quickly looked around and couldn't help but notice a large wooden packing crate behind the array of test equipment. He went over for a closer look; on the attached shipping slip it had USDOE, LANL, Los Alamos, NM, USA, Attn: Top Dog. So, thought Madison, they're sending it to the USA. Next to the crate were its lid and a pile of paper straw packing.

Suddenly Madison had a devious thought. He quickly looked around and spied a water cooler over by the wall. He went over to pick up the spare bottle of water sitting on the floor. It was too heavy for him to lift, so he tipped it over and rolled it to the crate. Next, with much struggling and straining, he rolled the thing up the lid and into the crate, covered it over with the paper straw and closed the lid. Let them analyse that, he thought.

He turned and began making his way back to the roller door, then stopped. There, on a nearby workbench, was the technician's lunch. Could it get any better than this? Madison thought. He quickly grabbed the apple and cookie and shoved them in his pocket. He then took the sandwich and munched his way back to the roller door and out into the car park. Once outside and clear of the building, Madsion turned, looked up at IQ's ship and gave the thumbs-up sign, with an extra big grin.

While all this was going on, IQ was following the events as they unfolded. He observed Madison go into the workshop and place the telesender from the see-through-things camera, and the navcom managed to pick up on what the Star Tracker was doing.

It became evident that the Star Tracker was indeed helping Madison, as it was causing mayhem with the complex's security system.

IQ correctly guessed that the telesender was in position and instructed the computer to activate it, half expecting to telesend Madison back into the ship. From his position in the car park, Madison could see the rock through the open roller doorway, and right on cue, it suddenly disappeared from the trolley. He looked up, gave another thumbs-up sign and emphasised the momentous event with another deliriously demented expression. Madison's face then turned serious. He reached in the pocket of his trench coat and held up another object, hoping IQ would see it. It was the remote to George's old TV. The odds were on his side this time; he hadn't confused it with the telesender.

"'Scuse me," a voice called out from behind. "Have you got a reason to be here?"

Madison turned. The gatehouse guard was walking over from the substation.

"Well, I live here," Madison replied.

The guard stopped in front of Madison. "You live here? Here in the Scientific Research Centre?"

"Oh no. I live here on Earth," Madison explained in all seriousness, emphasising the point with a sweep of his arm with a sandwich-filled hand on the end of it. He then took a bite and munched at the guard.

"Ah, smart arse, eh?" the guard said.

Madison turned round to see who the guard was referring to behind him, then turned back looking perplexed when he realised no one else was there. Just then a car horn beeped at the gate; the electricity service vehicle was waiting to leave at the exit barrier.

"If you have no business here, I suggest you leave before I call the police," the guard said, returning to his post.

"Righto," Madison replied. And he slowly shuffled out of the compound and into the street.

IQ didn't see Madison holding up the TV remote, he was too ecstatic about checking on his Y2K and getting it to the engine bay. This he did via a transportation duct that ran the full length of the ship, under the floor. The loading mechanism then guided the Y2K into the energy transference receptacle – or fuel tank – a slick operation that made intricate Swiss engineering look like a Heath Robinson contraption.

So far, so good, thought IQ. He returned to the flight deck, plopped into his seat and checked the fuel gauge. He stared at it. What a beautiful sight – the needle was on the F. He was all set.

The navcom then pointed out that the Star Tracker had disappeared.

Back at the Summer Sizzler gig, the punters were beginning to get stuck into refreshments and souvenir buying before the performances got underway. George and Steve were into their coffees at one of the outside tables by the time Charley arrived at the Sizzler Café.

"Hiya," she said. "You guys all ready?"

"Yeah," Steve replied. "Nothing that a few incompetent stagehands can't organise."

Charley asked George, "What were you on about before?"

"We had a run-in with the Star Tracker thingy," George explained. "It was lurking around stage right, but when we approached, it disappeared."

"Yeah. George scared it off," Steve said with a laugh.

"What?" said Charley, quite astounded. "What's it doing here? Is it following you?"

"I dunno," George replied. "I dunno what it's doing. Madison might have an idea."

"I wonder if it'll be back," said Steve, looking around. "Hey, maybe you should ask it to float around the stage while we're on."

"Oh yes, very Pink Floyd," George replied. He gazed thoughtfully into the distance. "I wonder if it has a mirror ball attachment."

Just then Matt and Razor turned up, both looking suitably attentive.

"Hey man, I tell ya, we're pumpin'!" Matt greeted excitedly.

"You two been into the pure oxygen?" Steve asked.

"Yeah, man. They gave us a few free puffs. Wakes you up, eh," Razor laughed. "Might be able to play now."

"Without making any mistakes," Matt added.

"Yeah, man. You should give it a go," said Razor.

"Well, there's plenty of it out here," said George, indicating the air. "You just have to breathe it in, you know? Easy when you know how."

"Yeah, nah, mate. This is one-hundred-per-cent oxygen, man. Gives your brain a boost," Matt replied.

"Well I'm sure that would be of use to you," George replied dryly, then added, "You know the Apollo One astronauts died in it."

"Eh?"

"When they were going through their launch practice runs in the lead-up to the moon landings, they had pure oxygen in the cabin," explained George, the all-round expert on such things. "And an electrical fault sparked a fire. Pure oxygen burns really well."

"Thanks for that gem of information, George," said Razor with a laugh.

"But that moon landing stuff, that didn't happen, did it?" Matt said.

George turned to Matt with a scowl. "Course it did!"

"Nah," Matt went on, "it was all a conspiracy. All done in a Hollywood studio. And the acting was so bad, everyone thought it was real."

The others laughed – all except for George who was annoyed. "That's bloody bollocks; of course it was real!"

"Well how come no one has ever seen the stuff they left up there?" Matt argued.

"Two reasons," asserted George, counting off on his fingers. "A – you're talking shit. And B – well there is no B – A covers it all."

"That makes sense," Razor said.

Matt glared at him. "Whose side are you on?"

"Well, what're you going to tell us next? The world is flat?" Razor asked.

George continued, "NASA's taken tons of photos of the Apollo landing sites with their Lunar Reconnaissance Orbiter."

"Well, that's very convenient, isn't it?" Matt argued for the hell of it. "Course they're gonna say they took the pics. Someone will go up there one day to the spot where they said they landed and there'll be nothing there. I'll put money on it, mate."

George shook his head. "The only place where there's nothing there is between your ears. Anyway, we all know you're talking shit."

Matt was well past the point of no return on the silliness stakes. "If you're so sure, let's put money on it. Come on, fifty bucks."

"Fine, you're on," said George, determined not to back down.

Steve acted as mediator. "Right, we're all witness to the great conspiracy debate between Matt and George," he said jokingly. "Drummer versus keyboardist. Someday their wisdom will be proven one way or another." He held up his coffee as if proposing a toast.

"By the time it is, fifty bucks will be worth fuck all," said Razor.

"It's worth fuck all now," said Steve.

Charley chipped in. "I think you need to stick to

drumming, Matt. Conspiracy theories aren't one of your strong points," she said with a laugh. "Anyway, it's not worth arguing with conspiracy theorists."

"Except that those who think it's a conspiracy are *wrong!*" George sneered at Matt.

Matt persisted. "And anyway, they couldn't have got into orbit because the Earth is flat ..."

The others laughed and shouted at him to shut it.

Charley could see George was annoyed. She reached over the table and patted his hand. "Aw, who's all upset about the poor old astronauts?" she joked with mock sympathy.

"Yeah, well," said Steve, looking to change the subject. "At least it's a nice day for it."

"So, we're on at one-fifteen, right?" Razor asked.

"Yep," Steve replied. "Make sure you're backstage half an hour before."

"That's quarter to one," Razor explained slowly to Matt. "When the big hand is on the ..."

"Oh is it?" interrupted Matt sarcastically. "They're always bloody late anyway."

"You guys will make up time," George said. "After getting pumped on pure oxygen, your tempos will be double."

"Nah, we'll have a smoke before. Mellow out, eh," said Matt.

Charley shook her head and laughed. "You're an odd one, Matt," she said. "Pure oxygen one minute, smoke the next."

"Yeah, why bother with all this air stuff?" Steve said, motioning at the air.

"Aw, come on," Matt complained. "You gotta give me some credit – at least I don't vape."

"True," Steve agreed.

"I think I'll go and have another shot of O2," Matt said. He got up to go. "Coming?"

"Yeah, why not?" Razor replied. "At least it's not bad for you. If we bump into any astronauts, George, we'll send 'em your way."

"Just don't inhale pure oxygen and light up at the same time," Charley called after them.

"Yeah, save it till your act," George called.

With Matt and Razor gone, the three could talk aliens.

"Have you heard from IQ?" Charley asked George.

"Not since last night. He's probably still in the reserve. I'll race down after this."

"I'll come," Charley suggested. "I can give you a lift."

"Cool," George replied. "I was hoping to demo SoundLive at some point, so sometime after that."

"Sure. What are you up to after this, Steve?" she asked.

"Just sorting the gear out. Get it back to the practice room. You two go along and I'll catch up later. You'll also have to find out what Madison's been up to, won't you?"

"Oh yes, Madison," said George, with a bemused look. "I stopped by his digs yesterday. He has quite a set-up, hidden away there behind the hospital. But he was telling me he owns a house, up in Browns Bay, but chooses not to live there – he rents it out."

After a slight pause, Steve asked, "Do you believe him?"

"Well, I guess. Oh, he said the Star Tracker dropped by as well, just before I came round. He was quite excited about it."

"I can understand that," Steve said.

"Did he say what it was doing?" Charley asked.

"No, he said it was hanging around outside. But when he went to show me, it had gone."

"Must have seen you coming," said Steve. "Uh-oh, here comes the cerebral one, I'm outta here," he laughed.

"We should have a little talk with Madison. I think he knows more than he lets on," George said.

"Either that, or he's completely mad," Steve said.

"Eccentric," Charley corrected.

"He is that," Steve agreed.

"Well, aren't we all?" said George.

"Absolutely. Here's to eccentricity," Steve said, raising his coffee cup.

Charley then said thoughtfully, "I wonder if we can talk to IQ at some point about how his life on ... where's he from?"

"Sirius C Major," George said.

"How it differs from our life on Earth. And if he can suggest how we could make our lives better," she said.

"Yeah, I hope so," George agreed. "I'd like to talk to him more about their technology, too."

"Why did he want your TV?" Steve asked.

"Gosh, I don't know," George replied, a little exasperated. "But I'm happy to give him a souvenir from Earth to take back. Even if it is a piece of shit."

"That was probably the last CRT TV left in the whole world," Steve said. "It's probably worth a fortune, and you've given it away."

George laughed. "I'm pretty sure there's loads more out there. Actually, that's a point – I wonder if he wants any more."

"We could go into business," Steve suggested.

"Intergalactic Traders!" Charley suggested.

"That's good!" said Steve, pointing at Charley. "I like that. What other junk could we flog him?"

"That reminds me," George said, "Madison was tidying up his digs when I went round to see him. He's got crap everywhere. All sorts of junk. He says he sells it. Anyway, he seemed quite particular about sorting it out."

"He's doing a garage sale?" Steve asked. "Or maybe opening a department store?"

"No, more like preparing for something." George thought for a minute. "He said something like he has to get ready."

"Ready for what?" Charley asked.

"I don't know."

"I think you're right," Charley said.

"What?"

"We need to have a little chat with Madison."

The car turned right into the street, and once again Reiner reeled as it headed for the left side of the road. Foley merely had her eyes closed. They continued on for a bit, and Reiner couldn't help noticing an old, scruffy-looking guy in a big coat wandering on the footpath, heading in the opposite direction. The guy grinned and waved at the car.

"Is he a friend of yours?" Reiner asked the driver.

"Is who?" the driver replied.

"Never mind," Reiner said. He could only guess that the guy probably waved at every car.

They pulled into the Scientific Research Centre driveway and stopped at the gatehouse barrier arm. The driver opened his window and handed a paper to the guard who studied it with deep interest.

After waiting a few seconds, Reiner called out, "US Agents Reiner and Foley to see John Davies."

The guard looked up and surveyed the car interior. "Oh yes. Project X, right? Visitor parking is outside the entrance," he said as he pointed the way.

The barrier arm went up and the car made its way across the car park.

"Project X," Reiner muttered. "Even the gate guy

knows about it."

They entered the building, John Davies met them at reception and they were issued with security passes.

"I understand this rock of yours is gaining a bit of interest," Reiner asked.

"It's interesting all right," Davies said. "Mysterious, might be a better word."

"Do we have any idea where it's from?" Reiner asked.

"We can only guess at the environmental and geological conditions of its origin, but it could be anywhere."

"But definitely extraterrestrial?"

"Oh yeah. Right this way."

He led them down the corridor and managed to get them through the various controlled doorways with no hassle at all. "Strange, these were playing up this morning," he said, gesturing at the door control. "Seem OK now." They entered the warehouse. "This is it."

They walked over to the middle of the room where all the instruments were grouped and the large wooden crate sat on the floor nearby.

"Packed up, is it?" Davies asked technician Simon Cooper.

Simon shrugged. "Looks like it." He bent down to remove the lid from the box and scooped out a bunch of paper straw.

The group stood in stunned silence, looking into the box.

"Well, this is mysterious," Reiner said dryly.

"What's this?" Davies demanded.

"Houston, we have a problem," Simon said as he began to frantically look around the warehouse.

The warehouse was fairly featureless; there wasn't anywhere the rock could hide.

"We need to find out what's happened here," Davies

said. "Do we have security video?"

"Yep," Simon said as he dialled his phone. "Roger. You far away? We need some help here. It appears to have disappeared." He hung up. "Roger Mora's on his way. I'll get him to work on the video footage. In the meantime, if you'll excuse me, I'll set up a search of the rest of the site." He hurried out.

Davies gestured at the box. "Some joke."

A thought struck Reiner. "That guy who waved ..."

"What about him?" Foley asked.

"Well, he seemed to think something was a joke. Foley, you stay here; I'm going for a quick ride."

Davies and Foley stood idle, both vacantly looking around the room. Eventually their eyes met. Foley raised her eyebrows and sighed. It was part of her job.

Chapter 21

IQ felt good sitting in his pilot's seat knowing things were back to normal. He could now go anywhere, do anything and, best of all, not have to bump into anyone.

Although he'd freely admit that George and the gang were helpful in getting him on his way, he wasn't about to dish out any medals. This is typical rev behaviour; they don't tend to give credit where credit's due. That's not to say they're ungrateful, it's just that once a job is done, no matter who does it, it's done. Move on. Next.

Of course, IQ had formed his own impressions of Earth and human behaviour, but he wasn't particularly judgemental about it. This is also typical rev behaviour. He'll say what he thinks of the human race, but only if asked. And even then, he won't say if it's good or bad. Revs will call a spade a spade, if they knew what a spade was, but only if asked.

But he was glad to be on his way. He'd gleaned enough from what life is like on planet Earth from his own experience and from what the navcom told him. That was enough as far as he was concerned. Curiosity is not one of revs' typical traits. But getting back to normal life was reassuring for him, even if it was ninety per cent sitting around in his spaceship by himself. Space travel was his life. It was in his blood. There was nothing more satisfying than cheating the laws of physics in getting from A to B.

At this point, he wasn't reflecting on recent events or reminiscing about his time with George and the gang. He was looking forward to what would happen next.

He was whizzing past Jupiter when he decided to go and look at his latest acquisition – George's TV. He left the flight deck and entered the lounge. The TV was suspended in the middle of the room with its back cover removed. IQ rotated it by dragging his finger on a nearby console touchpad. He could then study the insides of the TV and wonder what all the fuss was about.

The navcom advised, *The usual interface for the average star translayer is a low-frequency light-wave transmit device.*

IQ asked, *Is the TV's remote suitable?*

It is not only suitable, but absolutely essential in translayer operation.

IQ ho-hummed at this rather dull dialogue as he casually browsed the room for the remote. *Where is it?* he asked.

In Madison's coat pocket, came the answer.

Another typical rev trait is that they don't get violent; it's just not in their nature. They get frustrated, but they would never take their frustrations out physically on any living thing or inanimate object. This was just as well, for the sake of George's TV and anything within IQ's reach. For at this precise moment, IQ went through the rev equivalent of throwing a tantrum.

He took a firm grip on the edge of the console. He closed his eyes, bowed his head slightly and groaned for a few seconds. That was it; a perfect example of a rev losing his temper.

The navcom took no notice at first, partly because this was nothing out of the ordinary, but mostly because it was too busy working out how to get home without hitting anything.

Tantrum over, IQ quickly hurried back to the flight deck. He plopped in his seat and calmly told the navcom to turn around.

Madison made his way from the Scientific Research Centre back to his home at the edge of the reserve, a journey made quicker by use of the city's free tram. He was a frequent flyer on the tram and especially liked the free bit. Even if he had nowhere in particular to go, riding on the tram was a great way to pass the time and meet people. He liked to display a healthy demeanour by cleaning his teeth at fellow passengers – even though the rest of him looked a jumbled mess.

With the Scientific Research Centre mission behind him, he could now concentrate on what would happen next. He was completely oblivious to Reiner's frantic instructions to his driver in trying to backtrack and find him. But by that stage, Madison was on the tram and racing away at a blistering seven kilometres an hour.

Reiner and his driver circulated the neighbourhood a few times but eventually gave up and went back to the research centre, where tempers were fraying.

Once Agent Roger Mora got there, however, he calmed the group down and they started making some progress. It just took a few phone calls. He called the university and spoke with Hal Dawson and Dr Segway, and that uncovered two leads: Charlene Dibble and George Haley. Rick Wakefield was consulted and he put them onto Scotty, who, over the phone, said something like, "Ah ye cannae meake oos gruss on eh met, ya wee radgy fook. Wa ye teak mae for eh? Awae w ye."

Mora hung up, looking puzzled. "Um. If I'm not mistaken, I think he said George is indeed at the music festival."

Meanwhile, Madison arrived at the reserve and wandered down to the clearing, mumbling at random things along the way. Sure enough, IQ's ship was parked there. He waved and grinned madly.

The ramp lowered and Madison shuffled aboard. He made his way to the flight deck, sat down on the side couch, reached into his pocket, pulled out a half-eaten sandwich and offered it to IQ. After no reaction, he began munching.

IQ watched him from the pilot seat and patiently waited until Madison was settled. "Can you hand over the remote please?" he asked nicely.

"What remote?" Madison asked, innocently looking around.

"George's TV remote, the one in your pocket."

Madison searched his coat pockets and eventually pulled it out. "Oh!" he gasped, genuinely surprised that he had it on him.

IQ held out his hand.

But Madison clutched the remote to his chest, his eyes wide in his usual spooked expression. "The FBI are after George and Charley," he explained, as if it was a world conspiracy. "The agents are looking for the rock and they're after you, too. Secret agents, you know. Oh yes. And they know about the Star Tracker, too." Madison paused, scanned left and right, looking very spooked indeed. "Don't you see?" he whispered, "they can use the Star Tracker against you."

He'd invented this last point; it was worth a try, he thought. He knew IQ could easily take off and forget all about Earth. George, Charley and Steve would just have to take the rap from the authorities. But none of this was IQ's concern.

However Madison also had an ulterior motive. He'd made interstellar contact a number of times over the years and, as far as he was concerned, he was therefore highly experienced in such matters, and he felt this was his calling, his mission in life, to boldly go, as they say. Exactly how he was going to achieve this, he wasn't sure yet, but he was working on it.

IQ sat back in his seat and consulted with the navcom for a moment then turned to Madison. "Where are they now?"

Madison suddenly panicked. "Who?" he blurted, glancing around.

"George and Charley," said an exasperated IQ.

"Oh. I don't know," Madison said as he relaxed a little. Then with a sudden jolt, "The concert! What's it called? The summer thing! Yes, that's it!"

No sooner had Madison finally stopped gibbering, than a bird's-eye view of the Summer Sizzler stadium appeared on the screen. IQ took the ship down until they could get a clear view of the main stage. Of course, at this point, no one in the crowd even remotely suspected that a spaceship was hovering over their heads.

However, the ship suddenly stopped descending and quickly rose. The navcom pointed out the sound level was interfering with the not-be-seen sensors. If they went any closer, they'd run the risk of being seen. It could be a problem.

Madison was looking out the window and noticed that hot dogs were $7.50.

The plan was for George to demonstrate SoundLive early in the day, while the lower order bands were on. He wanted to get it out the way before Dark City's set. At midday, he went to the VIP tent in search of any amount of music industry people that he understood were going to be there.

He had his laptop with him, and the plan was to patch into a slave PA in the tent. He was hoping the event director had spread the word and the place would be buzzing with anticipation.

His backstage pass included VIP tent access, and he showed it to the two security guys at the entrance, who were actually more interested in watching a bunch of girls on the bungee swings nearby.

Once George entered the tent, he could see why; there were very few people in there. Just a vacant bar and someone dressed up in a bunny costume doing silly dances in the middle of the floor. The music over the slave PA was not what was going on onstage, but some stupid commercial tune about how dancing bunnies make all the difference in selling stuff; one of the sponsors, George figured.

At the far end of the tent, a huge LED screen showed live video of the main stage but without the sound. He looked around for the event director but couldn't spot him.

After meandering around for a bit, he came to the conclusion that he was in the wrong place. He hurried out and over to the mixer tent where he finally spotted someone he recognised: Scotty – doing some freelance work on the main sound desk.

God knows how Scotty got the job as lecturer at the university, George thought. Very few people could understand him. But George had an ear for the accent and the two got on pretty well. There were many foreign lecturers at uni and George had always felt that, believe it or not, you could do a lot worse than Scotty.

George leaned over the outboard racks and yelled at him. "Yo, Scotty!"

"Aye, Georgie boy. Hosey goin', bonny lud?"

George got straight to the point. "You seen the event director? I'm supposed to do a SoundLive demo."

"Oh, aye, ye goh eh goin' thun?"

"Yeah, I'm supposed to demo it to some VIPs, but I don't know where everybody is."

"Comb rownd." Scotty signalled George to squeeze past the end of the racks, and George bustled his way into the tent.

"I've got my laptop, and I was going to demo via a Wi-Fi link to a digital mixer on a slave PA in the VIP tent. I thought it was for around midday, but no one's there."

Scotty yelled at his assistant, then turned back to George. "Sorry, mon, I dannae naw warey is. Hang on a wee mo." He reached for his RT and yelled into it. "Eh Jimmeh, ya wee bustud. Ye naw ware Stansfield is, mon?"

George couldn't make out the garbled reply.

Scotty turned back to him. "Sorry, mon, a daunt naw. Eh, waa don ye 'ang arownd 'ere for eh but?"

"I'll have another look in the VIP tent," George yelled. "If I have no luck, I'll come back."

"Aye."

George started to take off when Scotty yelled after him. "Hey, George. Ye naw anything aboat thae SIS aftae ye? Ah goat eh call frome thae SIS, mon. Ah said nowt."

George stared at Scotty for a second. One thing at a time, he thought, then ran.

This time, George ran straight past the VIP tent security and both security guards reacted.

"Oi ,mate!" One of the guards ran after George and collared him. "Hey, you got a pass?" he asked.

"Yep," George replied and showed him. "I'm supposed to do a sound demo in here. Do you know where the event director is?"

"I think he's in one of the corporate boxes in the main stand. But you don't have access," the guard said, looking at George's pass.

"What's the best way to get a message to him?"

The security guard wasn't interested. He looked around and muttered, "I dunno." He started to go back to his post and said over his shoulder, "Try the stage manager, backstage."

George was getting annoyed. It would take ages to go backstage and look around. He decided to keep an eye on the VIP tent from the vantage point of the mixer tent, and he wandered back to rejoin Scotty.

"Ya fownd him, thun?" Scotty asked.

"Nah," George replied. He stood at the side of the mixer tent, staring at the stage, hands in his pockets and looking rather dejected.

"Aw, ne'er ye marnd aboat thaws bawzaws. 'Ere, lut's halve eh wee luke ut it, eh?"

George's face brightened. "Oh yeah, sure." He pulled the laptop out of his satchel, opened it and booted up SoundLive. "This is the main page," he explained. "From here you can select live control, saved settings or set-up. So from the live control screen, you can do all the usual mixing stuff including effects loops. I've just got a simple multi effects plug-in on this. Anyway, it communicates via MIDI, Bluetooth or Wi-Fi using MIDI commands. See, it's picked up your Wi-Fi link. Obviously you need a digital set-up controlling the PA; either a computer-based system or digital mixer."

"Aw aye, weh goat thart," Scotty replied, pointing vaguely at the sound control set-up. "Shall weh halve eh wee gaw, thun?"

"Try it now?"

"Aye. Art thae breck. Win thaes fookers ah fooked off," Scotty said, nodding at the stage.

"Yeah, cool," said George. "Got your Wi-Fi password?"

"Aye," Scotty said, and he reached under the desk and brought out a sheet of laminated card. "Here ye gaw."

George began punching in the code. "Hey, this has got Stanfield's number on it," he said, pointing at the card.

"Aye, thae wee fooker."

"I'll give him a bell." He whipped out his mobile phone. Stanfield's voicemail came on straight away and George left a message. "He's either on the phone or has it turned off."

"Aye. Towel thae fooked op fooker tae fook off," Scotty tactfully suggested.

The current band onstage finally finished and George fired up SoundLive. Scotty played back a multitrack recording of one of the day's earlier bands so George had something to play with. They had about twenty minutes before the next band was on.

"It's basically just MIDI control," George explained. "I've got a few system-exclusive commands that require an OS update on the host, but we can get by with this little demo by just using the basic commands."

"Och, aye," Scotty said as he followed George's explaining. "Ah lark ye wee knobs."

While the crowd sorted themselves out between acts, George took Scotty through the demo and the music over the PA changed all over the place while George did his tweaking. It was at a suitably low level, so no one really noticed.

Meanwhile, in one of the corporate boxes, midway up the main spectators' stand, the event promoters, including the chief director, Max Stansfield, and other music industry moguls were just gearing up for their obligatory gourmet buffet lunch complete with chilled champagne, courtesy of the event committee's lavish entertainment budget. Just then, two men and a woman, all wearing business attire, dark glasses and earpieces entered.

"Mr Max Stansfield? I'm Roger Mora, Foreign Liaison Officer with the Security Intelligence Service." He flashed his ID card. "These are Agents Will Reiner and Dianne Foley, FBI."

"That's nice," Stansfield replied, smiling, thinking it was a joke.

"We believe you have a George Haley working here on the sound crew. Can you point us in the right direction? We need to have a few words with him."

"Sorry mate, no idea," Stanfield replied. "You'll have to talk to the stage manager. Have you got a backstage pass?"

"No."

"How did you get in?" Stansfield demanded.

"We have police clearance," Mora said.

"You mean a warrant?"

"Not exactly. SIS directive. It's an urgent government matter. But the police have been informed and are covering all exits."

One of Stansfield's team sidled up and said, "George Haley was the guy who wanted to demo that sound control app."

"Oh yeah," Stansfield replied. "When is that happening?"

"I don't know," his friend said. "Stage manager would know."

"Yeah, you'll need to go backstage," Stansfield said. "Terry, can you escort these guys backstage?"

"Yeah, sure," Terry said.

Stansfield turned to the agents. "Do you fancy some lunch?"

"No thanks, we'll get on our way if we can," Mora replied.

Reiner then asked, "Mr Stansfield, have you been aware of any unusual or unexplained activity here today?"

Stansfield began to smile, suspecting it was all a prank. "No."

"We'll go backstage," Mora said hastily and ushered the group towards the exit.

Terry leapt to the lead. "Right this way."

Dark City hit the stage to an intro of rumbling sub-bass and a brassy synth riff played by George. The drums kicked in a thunderous beat and then Steve and Razor came bounding on, strapped on their instruments and laid into the first verse of their song of the moment, 'Getting There'.

Their set started swimmingly, and the crowd responded in a respectable manner. The sound balance onstage was fine and the group were feeling confident.

The end of 'Getting There' segued into another song; a simpler one in a lower key and a straightforward beat. Possibly not the ideal song to maintain audience attention as the crowd had got over the initial excitement of another band coming on and were starting to find other ways of amusing themselves.

The mosh pit was moshing continuously, whether there was music playing or not, and other punters inevitably began shouting conversations at each other or generally started to lose interest and wander away, and the crowd began to thin slightly.

Then the band started 'Black Star', and it immediately

got everyone's attention. Once the song got going, it was clear it was a winner. Punters were returning to the stage-front, hands were in the air, there was lots of yahooing and the mosh pit moshed furiously.

Steve glanced over at George during Razor's solo. "She's a good-un," he yelled.

George smiled back and managed not to make a mistake. He then noticed some business types watching from the opposite wing. They looked very secret-agent-like which was a good guess on George's part, because that's exactly what they were.

George was concerned that they were looking at him, although he couldn't tell for sure because they were all wearing sunglasses. However, he had an uneasy feeling that their presence might be something to do with IQ or the Y2K, or both. The rest of the band appeared not to have noticed them.

Suddenly, the sound changed. Wherever anyone stood or sat or moshed, no matter what position relative to the PA speakers or stage monitors, suddenly every punter, performer, sound engineer, stagehand, hot-dog seller – everyone – could hear Dark City's music in crystal-clear, perfectly balanced stereo hi-fi. It was if someone had just slapped sets of high-quality headphones on everyone's heads.

The sound was exquisite. It was precisely the sort of thing surround sound engineers strive for in the most expensive recording studios. It had a 3D quality to it, where different frequencies and dynamics seemed to find their own natural space, creating an overall perfect mix of aural brilliance.

Startled, the band looked round at each other, each thinking the other had made a mistake. Monitor engineers and stagehands stopped what they were doing and gazed around in disbelief.

From the mix tent, Scotty reacted in his usual fashion. "Fookin' 'ell!" he cried.

He wondered if he had dozed off and pressed the wrong button. He scanned the mixing desk and effects racks and then noticed George's laptop still patched into the Wi-Fi link. The laptop screen was alive with SoundLive activity. EQ graphs jumped up and down, parameters continuously adjusted themselves to optimum settings, virtual controls twisted and turned, spatial effects shimmered; it was as if there was a ghost in the machine.

"Fookin' 'ell!" Scotty blurted out again.

His first instinct was to switch the laptop off, but in the confusion he dithered. He stared at the screen, desperately trying to remember what George had said during his demo. A shape formed in the acoustic spatial window on the screen, a shape that was very spaceship-like. This didn't help Scotty one bit. He focused back on the mixing console, darted his eyes over the sea of knobs and faders, and eventually raised his vision towards the stage, and with a gormless expression muttered, "Fookin' 'ell."

Just as Scotty, the band, the audience and everyone else were trying to get their heads around this overpowering sound enhancement, a candy-apple-red spaceship suddenly appeared over the crowd. Or, at least, it would be candy-apple-red, if you could see it. Luckily George could.

Strangely, Reiner could also see it. "I take it that isn't your air force?" he said to Agent Mora.

"What?"

"We better make our move," Reiner yelled and hurried across the stage followed by Mora and Foley. They grabbed George and dragged him to the right wing while the band played on.

"George Haley," Reiner yelled above the noise, "I believe you know the owner of that extraterrestrial vehicle."

"Huh?" George managed.

"What are you talking about, Reiner?" Foley asked him.

Reiner continued to question George. "It's very important that we communicate with the occupier of that craft, urgently."

"What craft?" Mora yelled, looking totally confused.

"What?" cried George. "Who are you guys?"

The ship slowly and gracefully hovered towards the stage and George caught IQ's telepathic message; something like, 'I've got the Y2K. Madison is with me. Jump aboard.'

Mora tried a different approach. "George Haley, what do you know about the disappearance of the Project X asteroid from the Science Research Centre?"

"The disappearance of what?" George yelled.

"George, what's happening?" Charley cried out as she ran into the stage wing area.

The agents turned to face her.

"Charlene Dibble?" Mora asked.

"Yes?"

"Can you tell us the whereabouts of the Project X extraterrestrial asteroid? It was stolen from the Scientific Research Centre earlier today."

"Oh really?" Charley replied. "Last I saw it was at uni. When they took it out of the ground. Sorry, who are you guys?"

Reiner produced his ID. "FBI. We're here to accompany the Project X asteroid to the States."

George could see the end of the ramp near the front of the stage. Coincidentally, the dry ice machine was going nuts. He was going to have to make a run for it and drag

Charley with him. He only hoped he could still see the ramp when he got to it.

Meanwhile, in the mixer tent, Scotty was getting flustered over George's laptop. "Aw shit," he said. "Ah'll try thut button." He clicked on a control graphic with the mouse.

The three agents suddenly cringed and held their heads in pain as the band sound infiltrated their earpieces at full volume.

This was it, thought George, this was their chance. He grabbed Charley by the hand and took off towards the ramp. Charley needed no prompting; she was off like a rocket.

George wasn't sure if Charley could see the ship or not. He turned his head and yelled, "Jump!"

They both jumped together and landed on the end of the ramp, which then quickly withdrew into the invisible spaceship.

The three agents came staggering out to centre stage but were too late. George and Charley were nowhere to be seen. Steve and Razor suddenly appeared out of the clouds of dry ice and careered into the agents, sending them sprawling. Dark City played on, bouncing around the stage and playing their instruments like fury.

George and Charley flopped onto the couch on the flight deck. They were still holding hands and laughing at the mad panic getaway.

"Oh boy, that was crazy," Charley chuckled.

"It was!" George said with excitement. "Could you see the ship?"

"Not at first. Not until you said 'jump', then I could see the end of the ramp."

George realised it was quite a leap of faith for Charley, quite literally, and he felt glad she had trusted him.

They had another laugh about it, then George said, "Who were those suits? Cops?"

"SIS and FBI," IQ replied. "They're on to you two. They suspect Madison, too."

"What did he say?" Charley asked George.

George explained. It dampened the mood somewhat. Although, strangely, Madison wasn't bothered by it at all.

"But we haven't done anything," Charley said. "Not yet, anyway."

Madison piped up. "Oh yes we have. We've got the rock. Haven't we?" he said, grinning at IQ.

"That's great," Charley replied cheerily as the news brightened the mood again. "How did it go?"

"Oh, fine. Just fine," Madison replied, modestly.

"Cool," said George. "So what happens now?"

"They are going to be after you when you return home," IQ said. "We should try and clear your names."

"Oh," said George as the mood dropped again. "How are we going to do that?"

"We're working on it," IQ replied.

"Who? You and Madison?" George asked.

"No, I'm conferring with the navcom," IQ said. "Give me a minute."

There was a pause in the conversation. George glanced out the window and could only see cloud. He suddenly said, "Did you hear the music? It sounded amazing."

"Oh yes it did," Charley agreed. "How did it do that?"

"I don't know. I'll have to ask Scotty next time I see him."

"It was your program," IQ said.

George was shocked. "No!" he said. Then he suddenly remembered. "Oh shit, I left it patched into the main desk."

He mentally backtracked on the events. "The sound suddenly went, like, real hi-fi. Didn't it?"

"Yes, absolutely. It was great," Charley replied.

"But I can't imagine SoundLive making that much difference," George pondered.

"It did," said IQ, "with a few modifications."

"You modified SoundLive?" George asked.

"The Star Tracker did," IQ answered. "And it allowed us to get closer to the stage."

Just then a long string of computer code came up on the screen.

"There's the mod," IQ said.

George studied the code briefly. "That's amazing. Hang on. What are those characters there?"

IQ consulted the navcom for a second. "Option for infiltrating earpieces."

George sat back and admired the code. "Wow, that's brilliant. Incredible. But I don't know if I'll ever use the earpiece option."

"Well it's all on your laptop," IQ assured him.

"That's great. Thanks."

Charley was only getting half of the conversation. "What are you on about?"

George explained.

"You should get an A then," she said, truly happy for him.

"There are real commercial possibilities now," he said.

IQ didn't seem that bothered about SoundLive. He was still trying to figure out how they were going to deal with the authorities.

Just then Madison piped up. "I don't think we need to worry about that."

"About what?" George asked.

"The government, the secret agents," Madison said.

"Why's that?" George asked.

Madison thought for a minute. "I believe it is paying them a visit."

"Really?"

"Oh yes."

Charley gave him a quizzical look. "How do you know this, Madison?"

"It told me."

"When?" George asked, thinking it was like trying to get blood out of a stone.

"Yesterday. At the hospital. Just before you came round to my place. Remember?"

"OK," George said. "So what did it tell you exactly?"

"It zapped my mind!" Madison exclaimed, wide-eyed.

"Yeah, well never mind about that. How did you get the impression that it was going to sort out the agents for us?" George asked, desperately trying to be patient.

"It was more like a vibe, you know?"

"Yes, I know. It's given me a few vibes all right," George said.

Madison tried to elaborate. "I did get a message, but I can't remember exactly what it was. It's a bit like when you can't remember a dream when you wake up. But it all makes sense now."

George frowned. "Not sure if that's helpful or not."

IQ was silently in conference with the navcom. "The Star Tracker's still in the vicinity," he said.

A view of the backstage area came up on the screen. The group could see Steve, Matt and Razor being questioned by the secret agent types.

"George Haley and Charlene Dibble. Where did they go?" Mora asked the band.

Steve, Matt and Razor all shrugged and made 'I don't know' noises.

Reiner then said, "They appear to have jumped aboard an extraterrestrial craft."

The band looked at him blankly. Matt guffawed before

looking serious again. It seemed to be a serious situation, so it was best to look serious, he thought.

Mora screwed up his face at Reiner and said, "What the heck are you on about? There was no extraterrestrial craft."

"Sure there was," Reiner replied.

Foley piped up. "I'm not sure this is helping, Reiner."

"Just because you didn't see it doesn't mean it wasn't there." He turned to face the band. "You must have seen it."

Matt and Razor didn't want to say anything for fear of being drug tested.

At last Steve said, "Didn't see anything like that. We were concentrating on our set. You know?" He looked at Matt and Razor for support.

"Yeah, that's right," Matt said nervously.

"You must have seen or heard unusual phenomena," Reiner said. "Things you can't explain."

Just then, Steve noticed the Star Tracker droid positioned between two stacks of amplifiers. It had been sitting there talking to the dry ice machine. Steve figured its presence would provide a distraction, and a sudden thought occurred to him. He held up his arm and pointed. "You mean like that?" he said.

The three agents turned around. They didn't react until the Star Tracker began to move. It came out of its hidey-hole and gracefully floated around the stack of amplifiers and out the back of the covered backstage area. Stagehands, riggers, musicians all ignored it. Even the policemen ignored it at first. The three agents, however, suddenly turned into the Three Stooges. What followed would put the Keystone Cops to shame as the agents fell over each other in an attempt to apprehend the obviously extraterrestrial being.

"Agent Reiner, FBI," Reiner yelled at it, holding up his ID badge. "Stop right there."

Foley drew her gun and screamed at the top of her voice, "FBI! Freeze!"

The policemen suddenly jumped to action and joined in the chase. The Star Tracker was racing away across the grass area at the back of the stadium with the agents in hot pursuit. Suddenly it stopped and turned around. The agents came skidding to a halt, the policemen bumped into each other behind them.

"FBI!" Reiner and Foley yelled while wielding their handguns and badges at it.

"You are in direct violation of Federal law of the United States of America. You have the right to remain silent. Where is the Project X asteroid?" Reiner demanded.

The Star Tracker remained silent.

"What the heck's going on down there?" George asked, looking at the monitor screen.

"They're trying to arrest the Star Tracker," IQ said. "They think it's taken the Y2K."

"Well as long as they think that, we're in the clear, aren't we?" George suggested.

IQ didn't answer.

They watched for a few more seconds then suddenly George was excited. "Can you get us down there again?"

In no time at all, the navcom found a clear space on the grass and landed the spaceship.

"The ramp's down," IQ said.

"Come on, let's get back to the guys before the Feds return," George said. "Then they can't accuse us of taking off."

"Right," Charley said, jumping up.

"Wait for me," said Madison.

The trio headed for the door and ran down the ramp

and suddenly appeared out of thin air, if anyone had been watching, which, fortunately no one was, because the agents were providing all the entertainment. They were still trying to interrogate the Star Tracker, which by now was no longer floating – it was sitting on the grass, looking like a pile of scrap metal. Reiner put a tracking device on it.

"Someone's gonna claim it eventually," he reasoned. He then instructed the police to back off, put up some barrier tape, and observe from a distance. The strange thing was, it was more difficult to see from a distance. The Star Tracker had a knack of blending into its surroundings.

Meanwhile, George and Charley ran backstage, closely followed by Madison who was wishing he'd brought his rake along.

George spotted Steve and sensibly yelled, "Steve!"

The band had finished their set a few minutes before and were milling about backstage, the post-gig high dampened somewhat by the agents' actions.

"Hey, where did you guys get to?" Steve asked.

"Just act cool," George said. "When those agent types get back to us, let me do the talking."

"Yeah, sure. Anything we should know?" Steve asked.

"No," George answered vaguely.

"Hey, what happened to the sound?" Steve asked.

"Yeah, it was wild," Matt said.

"That was SoundLive, believe it or not," George said. "It was still patched into the mixing desk."

"SoundLive?" Steve asked. "You're kidding!"

"George Haley," Reiner called as the three agents came up the backstage stairs. "How did you get back so quick?"

"Back from where?" George said. "I was here all the time. We just did a gig."

"You entered that extraterrestrial craft and disappeared ..."

"There was no craft, Reiner," Foley interrupted wearily. "Let's get out of here."

"Listen," George said to them. "We've been here all day. Ask anybody. Check the security registration. Check the TV footage. We know nothing about that rock, other than it was removed from the university grounds the other day by some dodgy contractors."

"That's right," Charley said.

The agents could feel the trail going cold.

"OK," Mora said to the other two agents. "I'll go and check security and the TV. You go check your track and trace."

Reiner was visibly frustrated. He eventually flung up his arms in resignation. "OK. Fine." He turned to go with Foley in tow. Then he pointed a threatening finger at George. "The truth is out there," he said.

The band silently watched them leave.

"What a nutter," Steve said.

"Who were those guys?" Razor asked.

"Oh," George began, trying to think of a concise answer that would suitably summarise everything that had happened. "Secret agents," he said glibly, with a wave of his hand.

"Shall we get back to ...?" Charley said, motioning her head in the direction of IQ's ship.

"Yeah, we'll catch up with you guys later," George said. Then he realised someone was missing. "Hey, where's Madison?"

"You mean that funny old fella?" Matt asked.

"Yeah."

"He went that way," Matt pointed stage right.

Just then Madison came scrabbling through the stacks of amps, rigging and cables. "Where are they?" he said menacingly. He was holding a broom in his favourite attack position.

"Whoa!" Matt called as he backed off and held up his hands in mock surrender.

"It's all right, Madison, they've gone," George said.

Madison held his position for a few seconds. A confused look dawned across his face. "Who's gone?"

"The agents," George said.

"Agents?" he cried as he readied himself for the attack.

"No, they've gone," George explained. "Come on, let's go."

The gang went their separate ways. George held Charley's hand on the way back to the ship. He glanced over his shoulder occasionally to check that Madison was following with his broom. He suddenly felt he needed a lie-down.

Chapter 22

George, Charley and Madison sat on the side couch on the flight deck of IQ's spaceship. The mood was sombre. The elation of the post-gig high and escaping on the ship was rapidly fading. The fiasco with the agents was still cause for concern; they might yet be on their tail again.

IQ sat in his usual place in the pilot seat. He could sympathise with the group, but didn't. George had got himself and Charley off the hook for now, and that was fine with IQ.

Interestingly, the agents never found Madison. Even though he was the one caught on security camera at the Scientific Research Centre and the one Reiner saw and tried to chase. And his habitual desire to go scrounging prevented Reiner spotting him backstage. His choice of a broom as a weapon saved him again, because backstage security assumed he was part of the cleaning crew.

"So you got your Y2K," George said to IQ. "What do you want to do now?"

IQ stared at George for a moment. "I want to show you something."

George was suspicious. "It's not dangerous, is it?"

"You'll be quite safe in here," IQ assured him.

"He wants to show us something," George told Charley.

"That sounds ... interesting."

A minute later, Madison piped up, "That's where I live," he said calmly as he pointed out the window. The others turned to see Earth in the far distance.

"Holy shit!" George exclaimed. "Where are we going?"

Earth was getting smaller and smaller as they raced away from it. Out into open space.

The view was absolutely scintillating. They could see the universe in all its infinite, majestic glory. It had a very 3D look to it. They could feel the endless distance stretching out in all directions. The vast array of stars were shining brighter than they could ever imagine. They all made suitable 'ooh' and 'aah' noises as they glued their faces to the two small windows.

IQ couldn't see what all the fuss was about. "It's on the monitor," he said, pointing at the curved screen in front of him.

Suddenly, the moon came into view.

"Wow, look! The moon!" George enthused.

It looked massive. They were obviously getting very close and gaining quickly. It had only been a couple of minutes since they left the stadium. The ship tore around the moon in a suborbital trajectory, getting closer all the time. Soon their lateral movement slowed as the ship descended to the surface. Once they got closer, the crater-pocked surface sped beneath them, until finally the ship slowed right down and landed.

"Gee, that was quick," said George. "It took Apollo astronauts three days to do that."

"Actually, it was slow," said IQ. "But I wanted you to enjoy the journey."

"Where are we?" George asked, gazing out the window.

The landscape was desolate with no colour. George

was surprised they hadn't kicked up any dust. It was still and quiet.

"Tranquility Base," IQ replied.

"Apollo 11!" George exclaimed. He was getting very excited. "There it is!" he said, pointing out the window.

IQ had it up on the monitor screen, but the group found it more exciting to look at it directly through the window.

And indeed there it was. About 50 metres in the near distance, Tranquility Base, the bottom half of the Eagle lunar module, the instrument garden and the American flag, lying there from when it was blown over by the top half of Eagle taking off all those years ago.

George could make out hundreds of footprints all around the site. "Wow, that's so cool."

Charley turned from the window to smile brightly at George. She squeezed his hand. "There it is," she said, glad for him.

George couldn't keep his eyes off the scene outside. He was like a kid looking through a candy store window.

"Oh, it's the same as when it was on the TV," said Madison, reminiscing about the good ol' days.

"How do you mean?" Charley asked.

"Black and white," Madison replied.

"Oh yeah, it's stark all right," Charley agreed.

"Can we go out there?" George asked, without removing his face from the window.

"Why?" IQ asked.

"To walk on the moon!" George almost sang.

"It would be difficult," IQ said simply.

George didn't take that as a 'no'. He unglued his face from the window. "Can we do it?"

"No."

"Don't you have spacesuits?"

"Yes, but they won't be compatible. The bio-interfacing would be all wrong. It would take time to get it right and it would be risky," IQ said. "We can get a surface sample, though."

George was a tad disappointed in not being able to walk on the moon. He'd dreamed it often enough as a kid, but as he got older and wiser he figured that getting there would be fairly unrealistic. Now that he was there, his dream could still not be fulfilled. So close, yet so far, he thought. "Can we pick up a rock?" he asked.

"Yes," IQ muttered, a little bored. "We can pick up a rock."

A view of the moon surface directly under the ship came up on the monitor. The view panned and zoomed momentarily till it fixed on a suitable specimen. IQ then instructed the navcom to pick it up. This it did via the remote manipulator arm, which extended from a hidden hatch on the underside of the spaceship. With quick and accurate movement, the arm grabbed the targeted specimen and withdrew back into the hatch. IQ then instructed the navcom to repeat the exercise a few more times.

Finally he said, "It will be in the transfer bay." He got up and motioned George to follow.

The interior of the transfer bay was about wardrobe size, with gleaming stainless-steel-like lining and little in the way of detailed features. There were hidden panels in the floor and walls. One of these opened and IQ reached in and removed a stainless-steel-like tray, about shoe box size. He showed it to George.

"Fantastic," George said.

"Is this enough?"

"Yeah, I think so."

IQ carried it back to the flight deck, George following.

He handed the tray to George who gave out bits of rock to Charley and Madison.

"I'll save one for Steve as well." He turned to Charley. "What did Dr Segway say it was?"

"Some kind of basalt," Charley said.

"I think it's great," he said, admiring his rock. "What do you think, Madison?"

"Yes. Very special," Madison said. He studied it closely. "I wonder how much it's worth."

"It's priceless," George said. "Where else can you get this?" He handed the tray to IQ. "Do you want to keep a moon rock, IQ?"

"No."

George gave the rocks to Charley to put in her backpack. Madison pocketed his.

George suddenly had a curious thought. "IQ, was there anything you wanted to take back from Earth? You know, like a souvenir?"

"Yes," he said.

"What?"

"The Y2K."

"Apart from that," George said.

"The translayer."

"Apart from that. You know, like, I dunno ..."

"Like a record," interrupted Madison.

"A record?" George asked.

"Yes," said Madison.

"You mean an LP record?"

"Yes."

"Why?"

"They sent one up into space, didn't they?"

"They did! You're right, Madison," George said. "Yes, on the Voyager space probe." He thought for a moment. "Are distant aliens really likely to have a turntable?"

"How about if we take a photo?" Charley suggested as she dug her phone out of her backpack.

"Good idea," said George.

They all gathered around IQ and Charley did a selfie. "Smile," she said, even though revs were incapable of smiling. "Perfect. Do you want a copy?" She then asked George, "Does he want a copy?"

IQ stared at George for a moment. He didn't really want a copy, but he could tell they would be offended if he refused.

The photo suddenly came up on the monitor.

"Yay, it looks great," Charley said.

Suddenly they were moving. The starry background was whizzing by. On the monitor they could see the moon getting smaller and smaller at an alarming rate.

The group sat quietly as the mood dropped while they contemplated the inevitable parting of the ways. George and Charley were certainly going to keep seeing each other. Madison still had ideas in his head that he was about to go on a big adventure of some kind. IQ just wanted to fulfil his mission.

After a while, George broke the silence. "IQ, what are you going to do with my TV?"

"You mean the translayer?" IQ asked.

"Yes."

"Deliver it to a research organisation on Crux Alumina."

"And what will they use it for?"

"I've no idea," IQ replied. He couldn't be bothered asking the navcom.

George thought for a minute. "That's funny. We robbed a research organisation on Earth to provide for a research organisation on Crux Whatsitsname."

"Alumina," IQ corrected.

They landed in the reserve. IQ felt it was a safer spot, considering it was still daylight. It was nearly time to go, but George had all sorts of last-minute questions he wanted to ask. Things like: Do revs believe in God? Could humans live on the Sirius C planets? Can you show us how to build a spaceship?

In the end he merely asked, "Do you think we'll meet again?"

"No," IQ said. Blunt as always.

"You don't think you'll ever be out this way again?"

IQ thought for a second. "Not likely."

"What about the Star Tracker?"

"If it continues its usual pattern, it will probably be back," IQ replied.

"No, it won't," said Madison.

"It won't?" George asked. "How do you know?"

"I think it has all the information it needs," Madison replied.

"How do you know that?" George asked.

"Oh, well, I ..." Madison began. "... I just know," he said, looking at the floor.

Madison's usual straightforward answering technique, thought George.

He held out his hand. "Well, goodbye," he said to IQ.

IQ shook his hand. "Goodbye." He then shook Charley's and Madison's hand.

The three exited and walked down the ramp, waving and calling their final goodbyes. George led them over to the edge of the clearing where he stopped and turned around. IQ's ship wasted no time in taking off. In two seconds it was gone.

"He's gone," said the helpful Madison.

George sighed. "Yep," he said, and turned to walk up to the university.

Madison veered off down his path, and George and Charley entered the university grounds.

George paused at the courtyard. "Can you get home all right, Charley?"

"Yes, I can catch the bus. You?"

"Um ... yeah," George said, pondering his options. He put his arm around Charley's shoulders. "Quite an adventure, wasn't it?"

She looked up at him and smiled brightly. "Yep. Quite an adventure. Who'd believe it, eh?"

"I know ..." said George, a slight emotion creeping into his voice.

Charley gave him a hug. They embraced for a bit, with the recent events tumbling through their minds. For once, George wasn't worried what anyone thought as they passed by. Then, as if on cue, they looked into each other's eyes and kissed the longest, sloppiest kiss in the history of the universe.

At last, Charley said, "Come on. What do you say we go get a drink?"

"Good idea," said George.

The next morning, Madison shuffled into The Space Place Internet café at precisely six minutes past nine. This was perfectly reasonable, he thought, because it was four-dollar tea-and-muffin special between nine and ten. He ordered a cup of tea and slopped milk and three sugars into it. He made a fuss about choosing a muffin, and then went off to sit at one of the in-house terminals.

He logged on to eBay to check his listings. He often listed items he'd found in his meanderings around the city. He was quite pleased with his last item, a rake, which sold for five dollars.

This time, he had a particularly special listing: 'Moon Rock – From Tranquility Base'. The listing described it as the genuine article from the Apollo 11 moon landing site. Madison was pleased to find plenty of interest, and there were a few questions posted. He glanced down them but his excitement soon waned. To his surprise, people were making fun of it, with comments like, 'Been to a west-coast beach then?' and 'Who's a loony then?' and 'Yeah, I got one of those. Ha ha.'

Madison was about to begin answering them with utmost sincerity, when he suddenly had a change of heart. No, he thought. Maybe this one he'll keep for himself. He cancelled the listing and logged off.

He sat there staring at the blank screen. The café was fairly busy, and people were bustling back and forth on the pavement outside, with the incessant traffic cacophony continuing in its customary unabated fashion. People were going about their daily business as usual, and no one gave him any hint of acknowledgement that he was there, filling up space, if nothing else.

There was absolutely nothing to suggest to anyone that he had just been to the moon and back. Hurtling across the 200-odd thousand miles like it was a walk in the park. Forget mission control, forget Houston. Chauffeured by a gangly, moody, TV-obsessed, pot-smoking alien. Whip up, grab a rock or two, whip back, no problem. He suppressed the urge to jump up and tell everyone. But no, this was something he was going to keep to himself. Besides, he already knew no one would take the slightest bit of notice.

He took the moon rock out of his coat pocket and scrutinised it in his fingers. A nearby patron looked over to see what Madison had in his hands. Madison frowned at him, clamped the moon rock tight in his fist and put it back in his pocket.

He finished off his tea and gazed out the window at the busy city street. He vaguely noticed the headline at the newspaper kiosk. Something to do with government agents entertaining festival-goers. It failed to capture Madison's attention as the recent events played round in his head a bit more. He grinned at nothing in particular. He chuckled to himself and shook his head. A passer-by caught his eye and hurried on, looking rather startled.

He finally gathered himself together to leave. He went through his normal routine of checking his pockets, his toothbrush, his moon rock, buttons that needed to be buttoned up, woolly hat adjustments, and generally trying to give the impression he was preparing for a busy day of doing important things. But today was different. He could feel it. He knew this day was coming and he was ready.

As he stood up, he felt something strange in his pocket and pulled out George's TV remote. That's odd, he thought, because he was sure he'd given the remote to IQ. Even stranger, the remote appeared to be a fake; none of the buttons would push down. As he pondered this, he made his way slowly to the door and promptly vanished into thin air.

* * * * *

Thanks for reading
IQ and the Y2K.

Look out for the sequel,
available soon on Amazon.

* * * * *

Made in the USA
Middletown, DE
21 April 2021

37164163R00128